A Witch's Guide to Surviving Halloween

A Witch's Guide to Surviving Halloween

A COZY SMALL-TOWN ROMANCE

A M ENO

To the grandmas who made the holidays magical. To the friends who are like sisters and the sisters who are friends, you make this world a little easier to survive.

And a warning from my husband: do not read on an empty stomach. Story may cause hunger!

Chapter One

"Why do I live here?" Lucy grumbles from her perch, cross-legged on one of the pedestals to either side of Moonlit Pages's front stoop.

I have to hold back a giggle, burying my chin in the collar of my jacket, because she looks like a puffball in her checkered fleece coat. She pulls her hands into the sleeves, nothing but her clover eyes peeking over the top. The hood covers her bright red curls, casting her face in a very fitting shadow. Fishnet tights poke through the tears in the knees of her stone-wash jeans, white frayed edges fluttering in the crisp autumn breeze, making her shiver dramatically.

"Because you *love* Ashwood Haven," I tease, eyeing the jack-o-lantern nestled into the corner between the base of the pedestal and the bottom step, which had been sitting where Lucy sits now when I left the store last night.

Lucy scowls, tucking a stray ribbon of red hair back into the hood of her coat with a hand that pops up through the head hole. Heavily-lined eyes narrow at me and I can already tell she's beginning to question all her life choices, like she does every day, up to and including just how much she loves me.

"Nope," she bites. "Try again."

I step up onto the bottom stair of the bookstore and coffee shop, so we're eye to eye, and flash her a mockingly innocent smile. "Because you're too lazy to leave."

Rolling her eyes, she jumps down from her roost. Platformed books thud against concrete and she toes the carved pumpkin she'd unceremoniously dethroned. "Oh, right. *That*."

With a rustle of keys, I push through the paint-chipped front door, the bell chiming with our arrival at the already warm store. Lucy follows me in a rush, exaggerating her shudders as she stomps her feet and whips the empty sleeves of her coat back and forth. A wreath of cotton spider webs and plastic tarantulas interwoven with burnt orange and ruby-red leaves clacks against the glass pane of the door as I lock it. It's the same color as the turning leaves on the trees, evenly spaced down Main Street, the now balding branches swaying in the biting morning breeze.

Lucy turns and starts her morning waddle toward the coffee bar, holding her enchanted coat close. Charming the lining to keep her toasty warm on cold mornings like this was the first thing she did with every new jacket.

I, on the other hand, leave my jackets as is, letting the wind find its way through the weave of the wool, so I can bask in the autumn air.

"Oh, come on. Aren't you excited for the Halloween festival kick-off tonight?" I beam, my cheeks and nose still tingling from a chilly walk to the center of town. "A full week of bobbing for apples, hot cider, and donut booths? The parade?"

Lucy pouts at me, her bottom lip sticking out so far it's comical. "All the customers order the same pumpkin spice whatever, tourists are everywhere, and the air hurts my face."

I sigh, shrugging off my taupe coat and draping across the carved wooden desk that's as old as Ashwood Haven itself. I take care not to knock over the little plastic skeleton sitting on our card reader, patting it on the head when it stays upright. "You realize that as the person who runs the coffee bar, you could choose not to serve the pumpkin-spice-whatever drinks, right?"

"Yes," she whines, "but then *I* can't drink them."

I shake my head at her, a thin sympathetic smile at her early morning grumblings pulling at my cheeks.

"But the lantern walk?" I call to her retreating form, just to see her reaction, knowing full well she's always hated the lantern walk —even though it's one of my favorite festival activities.

Lucy throws her head back and groans. "Ugh!"

I giggle, leaning around a row of bookshelves to catch a glimpse of her staring down the espresso machine as if she's preparing to challenge it to battle. "Don't forget, we're staying open late all week and you're in charge while I'm gone."

"Not today, Satan," she yells back, not bothering to glance my way.

"That's Amelia to you."

"Same thing before eight."

Grinning to myself, I tuck a long black lock of hair behind my ear that's already come loose from my ponytail on my walk to the shop this morning. I wave a hand at the light switch, and half the overhead lights flicker to life, swathing the store in a warm glow that elicits a patented Lucy groan.

I leave her to stew in her pre-coffee petulance and start my morning routine to prepare the shop for a busier-than-usual day.

With the Halloween festival starting tonight, tourism numbers will be up, signaling the beginning of this year's rush. I take this time to enjoy the peace and serenity of having the bookshop almost entirely to myself.

My patchwork skirt brushes against my calves and I pull the cuff of my chunky knit sweater down over my hands despite the magic heating the store. In the years since I took over the shop from my grandmother, there have been a handful of spells I never touched, but this one is my favorite. Each morning, it feels like walking into one of her hugs, her reassuring arms wrapping around me from beyond the veil that separates the living from the dead.

Rubbing worn strands of yarn between my fingers, I do my best to ease the nerves, making my stomach churn at the thought of tonight's opening ceremony. Ashwood Haven's legendary week-long Halloween festival is my favorite celebration of the year, and I'm really looking forward to it . . . if I ignore all the things that make this year different.

With a deep breath, I push the butterflies down and spend the first hour before opening wandering between dark wooden shelves, occasionally rearranging a stack of tomes that jumped off the shelves in the night. Most sections are well-behaved, but the travel section is particularly restless for some reason. I tell them every night that they have to stay where I sort them. And yet, every morning, I find them scattered around the store.

I sigh as I discover yet another volume about castles in Ireland sitting in the fantasy section.

Grandma never had this problem; the books always listened to her. With a firm talking to and a wag of her finger, they would stay in their place every time. I, on the other hand, have to tote *Best Day*

Hiking Trails of the Southwest back from the geology section every morning.

Despite the ill-behaved books, this first hour before opening is always my favorite. Lucy and I work in silent companionship, doing our own thing together, and it gives me a chance to prepare myself for the conversations to come.

But at precisely eight o'clock, I brace myself and approach the front door. Through the glass, I spy an already waiting figure, swaying on his feet as he looks out over the main artery of Ashwood Haven, coming to life by the minute.

I wave a hand to light up the rest of the store and give myself my daily pep talk, convincing my nervous system that chatting with customers isn't a life-or-death situation. With only a mildly forced smile, I flip the sign on the front door from CLOSED to OPEN, turn the lock, and within seconds, the bell announces our first customer.

I step back from the door as Don steps through, his gregarious presence overwhelming in the way it changes the whole atmosphere of the shop. By simply stepping inside, he transforms the space from quiet and cozy to alive and boisterous.

"Good morning, girls!" he bellows, the same way he does every morning.

I push the door closed behind him, ensuring none of the warm air escapes. "Good morning, Don."

He tips his chin at me and beelines for the coffee bar, rubbing his large hands together to stave off the cold.

I follow close behind, plopping myself down on one of the stools lined up against the counter and swivel back and forth as I wait to hear this morning's town gossip.

"The usual?" Lucy asks, already pouring espresso beans into the grinder.

"Yes, ma'am. With an extra sprinkling of whatever it is you do that helps me sell the town to newcomers."

Lucy shoots me a look out of the corner of her eye before flipping through the spell book behind the counter, its pages yellowed with age and charmed to never tear. She grabs her mortar and pestle and starts grinding a mixture of allspice and cinnamon for a mix of luck and business success while mouthing the coinciding spell under her breath.

I rest my elbows on the granite counter, my chin in my hands as I lean in. "What's the big occasion?"

"Oh, a young man is opening up shop across the street. I want to make a good first impression when I welcome him here shortly." The announcement is boisterous, in the only way Don knows how to speak, but the way his mustache twitches at the end suggests an opinion on this whole matter that he isn't sharing.

"First impression?" Lucy raises a perfectly-shaped eyebrow at the half-bald man who practically runs the town. "He's opening a store downtown, and you haven't even met him yet? That's not like you."

"I'll be quite honest, girls, this is a bit of an odd one. I wanted to show him around town before he bought the shop, but he insisted he wanted that one and only that one. Nothing was going to change his mind. Miss Laura only had it up for a day before he bought it right up."

I tut my tongue. "Oh, Miss Laura. I can't believe she's retired."

"I can't believe her niece wouldn't come home to run the bakery. She grew up behind that counter." Lucy chimes in, lip curling with distaste.

I tip my head, my black ponytail swaying as I give her a scolding look. "She has a husband and kids in the city, not to mention her job doing . . ." I rack my brain, trying to think back to one of Miss Laura's many prideful laments about her niece's success, coming up short. "Whatever it is she's doing."

"See? Selfish."

"Miss Laura said she'd give you that apple fritter recipe if you wanted it," I remind her.

Lucy sighs, shoulders drooping with exaggerated exasperation. "It wouldn't be the same."

I roll my eyes at her, turning my attention back to Don. "So, is he going to keep it a bakery?"

"He is, actually. Said it's a family business."

Lucy thoughtfully hums as she finishes Don's drink off with a sprinkling of charmed spice powder.

"What?" I ask her.

"Well, you'd think a guy so interested in maintaining *family* tradition would take over a *family* bakery. If preserving heritage is your goal, why would you open one up somewhere new?"

I tap my fingernails against the countertop, using the tips of my brown wingtip boots to swivel back and forth on my stool. "Maybe he's looking for something new. Or someone else took over the family business, like a sibling. *Or* maybe it will be another branch of the family bakery."

"Maybe he's running away from something," she mutters, pushing the drink across the counter.

"Cynical much?"

Lucy raises her hands in defense. "It was just a suggestion."

"So long as he runs an honest business and doesn't cause any trouble, I'll be happy to have him," Don declares, grabbing his cup and raising it like a toast. "Speaking of the town"—he turns to me, taking on a more serious tone—"Miss Amelia."

I straighten, crossing one tight-clad leg over the other and matching his professional tone. "Mr. Don?"

"You're sure you're ready for tonight? Hosting Halloween is a lot of pressure around here, and most first-year business owners wouldn't be up for it. I know you were counting on your grandmother—"

I cut him off with a wave of my hand. My heart aches at the mention of Grandma, and I already know where this is going. It's only been a few months since she died. She was so excited when we found out Moonlit Pages would be sponsoring the festival this year, and we all thought she'd have one last chance to host her favorite event of the year, that she'd have one last Halloween with us. With her gone, though, the responsibility falls on my shoulders as the new official owner. I've more or less been running the store for a few years now, but it wasn't until Grandma passed through the veil of spirits that ownership formally passed on to me. Since then, it's been an endless stream of people asking me if I'm okay and if I'm ready to take on such a hefty responsibility. If I would like to pass off my hosting duties to someone who isn't going through the grieving process.

No matter how much I tell them all I'm fine, apparently there's still a question as to whether or not I can handle hosting such an event. It probably doesn't help that *I'm* questioning it as well, but I have to stay strong—if not for the town, then for Grandma. I want to do this in her honor.

So, I plaster on my brightest smile, unwilling to show him how the reminder of Grandma's absence, and all that comes with it, makes my stomach sour. "I'm sure. Grandma wouldn't have wanted it any other way."

Don presses his lips into a thin line, the grimace almost disappearing beneath the bushy mustache. "I know it's what she would have wanted, but if you aren't ready . . ."

I shake my head, holding my chin high and willing my shoulders back to portray a confidence I'm still trying to find. "I can do this, Don. I promise, I won't let you down."

"Oh, I'm not worried about that. I just know your grandmother left some pretty big shoes to fill."

I know his concern is nothing but kind, yet it feels as though he's slowly driving a knife through my heart. Every day without Grandma has been a struggle, but I've devoted every waking moment to ensuring things go on like normal, with minimal disruption to everyone's lives.

My shoulders begin to sag under Don's doubt and concern, and the steel rod I've tied to my spine since her funeral starts to bend. Maybe I haven't been managing things as well as I thought, especially if even Don can see through me so easily.

"Amelia is more than ready," Lucy butts in, noticing the way I'm starting to crumble. She puts on her signature smile that warns everyone within a mile radius that she's ready for trouble. "Besides, she has me backing her up. What could go wrong?"

Don puffs out his cheeks and blows a long breath through tight lips, giving a small shake of his head. "Yes . . . Well . . . Good luck with that, Miss Amelia." He leans across the counter, lowering his voice in a mock whisper. "Don't let her anywhere near the children's activities."

I giggle conspiratorially at Lucy's gaping mouth.

"Hey!"

Don gives me a wink and turns away, taking a sip of his drink. "Have a nice day, girls!"

I wave at his retreating back. "See you tomorrow."

The moment the bell above the door announces his departure, I slouch with relief, leaning against the countertop for support.

"Thank you," I mutter, all my forced congeniality palpably leaving my body.

"It's okay, ya know. To ask for help, show a little bit of vulnerability. Everyone knows how hard it's been for you since she died."

"I know, but . . ." I sigh, my chin thumping against my forearms. "I knew this was Moonlit Pages's year to sponsor the festival, but I thought she would be here. I thought I had one more Halloween with her. The planning was easy; I've been helping her with that my entire life. But the speeches, socializing, and all that . . . She would have loved doing it all one last time."

Lucy presses her lips together, emerald eyes studying my pathetically hunched form. "I know, it was sudden. Honestly, I thought the old girl would never die."

With the first smile of the morning, she dances out of reach as I swat at her. "Hey now, careful what you say. The veil between here and the afterlife is thinning every day; she'll probably hear you and hex your milk frother."

Lucy holds up a finger. "Don't you dare say that. Grandma," she calls out to no one in particular, "if you're listening, I'm sorry. We love and miss you. Please don't hex Milly from the afterlife."

A giggle bubbles out of my chest. "Milly?"

She pets the frother affectionately. "That's her name today."

"Yeah, well, yesterday it was 'that MF.' As in 'that motherfucking milk frother.'"

"All couples fight. Yesterday was a bad day, but we're starting over."

I can't stop the genuine chuckle that shakes my shoulder, and I'm reminded why I love this girl so damn much. The jangling front door announces our first actual customer of the day, and I jump to my feet, straightening my skirt.

"Time to get to work."

"Yay," Lucy grumbles, already preparing for her next drink order.

Chapter Two

Stepping back, I scrutinize the display table I've been arranging, tilting my head this way and that. Something about the display still seems . . . off. Halloween is all about fun and mystery, and everything here is too polished and put together.

I twist one of the apple cinnamon candles slightly to the left so the label is off-center, and then step back again. Pyramids of candles are nestled among autumn-colored silk leaves and flowers. Strands of cotton cobwebs are strung between branches I plucked off the sidewalk on my way to work yesterday, hung above plush black cats with purple pointed hats and a variety of crocheted ghosts. The whole thing is accented by the glow of orange and purple string lights hidden among the foliage, and I eye the ghosts again.

The little one with a purple and orange hat has been calling my name since the day Lila dropped them off to sell on commission. I make a mental note to buy it tonight if no one takes it today. It would be perfect on my bookshelf at home, its little smile making my heart melt.

Satisfied with the display, I turn to head back to the counter and run face-first into a broad chest.

"Oh!" I squeal, stumbling back.

A large hand catches my elbow before I run right into the table I've spent all morning working on and ruin my perfectly disorganized setup.

A deep voice wraps around me, instantly reminding me of a warm, steaming cup of coffee on a cold winter morning. "Careful."

"I'm so sorry," I mumble and do my best to regain my balance, inadvertently reaching out to steady myself against him before pulling my hand back just as quickly.

"No, I'm sorry. I should have said something before I startled you. I would have, but I thought you heard me come through the door." He jerks a thumb toward the front door with a still-swinging wreath. The movement emphasizes how his shoulders tug at the seams of his dark gray button-down. He's brawny in the way guys are when their muscles come from a need for actual strength, as opposed to those who work out for the aesthetic of it.

I let out a strained laugh, trying and failing to brush off the embarrassment warming my cheeks. As I do, I step away, putting space between us to ward off a shiver that skitters across my skin at his proximity. The feeling makes me twitchy, something familiar in the goose bumps that I can't put my finger on.

"I must have been lost in my own little world. Can I help you find something?"

A crooked smile lifts his cheek, a dimple revealing itself in a way that makes my heart stutter. Before I can stop myself, I press a hand to my chest, as if that will stop the strange feeling.

"Yeah, actually. A person. Don told me to come introduce myself to Miss Amelia, the owner."

Again, my heart squeezes, this time at the sound of my name on his lips. It's so unsettling, I try to remember all the signs of a heart attack the doctor told me to look out for when Grandma had her first medical scare. Does my left arm hurt? I've felt nauseous all morning, but I chalked that up to pre-speech nerves.

He eyes the way I'm pressing a hand to my chest. "Are you okay?"

I swallow hard and force a pleasant mask onto my face between one breath and the next, letting my hand drop to my side to try and hide my sudden discomfort.

"Yes, I'm fine." The words come out more exasperated than I intend, though I know it's not his fault, whoever he is. I've just repeated the words so many times I'm starting to think they'll be written on my gravestone when I finally die of exhaustion from saying them. So, instead, I add a cheery note to my words, in hopes he knows it's not him I'm irked by.

"You've found her. Amelia Nova, at your service." I give him my best customer service smile and run a palm over my skirt to smooth a non-existent wrinkle to distract myself from his steel blue-gray eyes.

Bemused, his head tips to the side, showing off a strong jaw and thick neck. "You're . . . Sorry, when Don said Miss Amelia ran the bookstore, I assumed you'd be . . ."

"Old?" I finish for him.

His gaze drops to the floor as he bites his lips, and I swear a hint of blush starts to color his cheek as he runs a hand through his golden-brown hair. "Yes."

I let out a lighthearted laugh, this time genuine, because I completely understand the confusion. "That's okay. Don calls everyone miss or mister; you'll get used to it."

We stand there for a moment, those blue eyes studying me with an intensity that has me squirming.

"So," I start, clearing my throat and straightening one of the candles a millimeter. He jumps as if he forgot we were in the middle of a conversation. "If Don sent you over, that must make you the guy who bought Miss Laura's bakery."

"Yes, sorry. I'm supposed to be introducing myself. I'm Oliver. I . . . bought the bakery, like you said." He presses his lips into a tight line, shifting from one foot to another. "I'm not doing a very good job of this."

I soften, ignoring the weird energy between us as sympathy warms my chest. Having never really left Ashwood Haven for longer than a vacation, I have no idea what it's like to be the new person in town. I imagine it isn't easy, no matter who you are.

"You're doing great." I stick out my hand. "It's nice to meet you, Oliver."

Thick fingers curl around my hand as our palms meet. Heat from his touch crawls up my wrist as he gently shakes my hand. "It's nice to meet you, too, Amelia."

For a moment, our connected hands hang in the open air between us. I meet those wintery eyes and lose myself in their glittering embrace. Their depthlessness could be pulled straight from the winter landscape of a Viking fantasy series, the one he seems to have materialized from, the precise color of an icy shadow.

Something in the air shifts. A static charge erupts around us, making the hair on my arms stand on end. The odd energy leaves an achingly familiar taste in the back of my throat; something I've experienced before, but never to this extent.

Suddenly, a quiet rattling from one of the nearby shelves catches my attention. It's subtle at first, like someone trying to loosen a sticky doorknob, but it escalates into a full-on quaking within seconds.

I drop his hand and dart around the end of a nearby shelf, Oliver on my heel, searching for the source of the shaking.

In the middle of the romance section, a paperback is inching its way off its shelf. I lunge for it, snatching it before Oliver notices it moving on its own.

The bookshop's magical tendencies and the depth of Ashwood Haven's witchy heritage aren't exactly a secret, but they also aren't advertised either. It's a history accepted by locals but brushed away from the prying eyes of tourists and newcomers.

Grandma wasn't subtle about charming her way into an easier life as the only still-practicing witch in town, with shelves that never collected dust and brooms that occasionally swept on their own after hours. She started teaching me the ways of my ancestors at a young age, with little opposition from Dad, who neither embraced nor denied our heritage.

When Grandma learned that Lucy came from a long-forgotten line of witches, she started including her in our lessons as well. Her number one lesson? Never be ashamed of our lineage, but always be thoughtful about who we share it with.

I cradle the paperback in the crook of my elbow, clutching it tight. It's still shaking, jerking in my grip with a concerning intensity. I scowl down at it and hiss at it to stop before turning to beam at Oliver, my forced smile returning.

"What was that?" His wintery gaze searches the empty space on the shelf for answers and runs thick fingers through his golden locks again. A line forms between his brows when he finds nothing but a blank wall behind the books instead of a person pulling a prank.

A nervous giggle bubbles out of me, and I can only hope it doesn't sound as jittery as I feel. "Just a precarious book. You know how customers are. They'll leave things anywhere, even on the edge of a shelf."

He side-eyes me warily, not fully convinced by my explanation. "That thing sounded violent, not loose."

I shrug, a wooden grin still stiff against my cheeks, when I spot another book starting to slide forward out of the corner of my eye. This time, it's right above his head.

Without thinking, I lunge forward and throw up a hand to hold the book in place, only to end up stepping right back into his personal bubble. Chest to chest, we're far closer than two strangers have any right to be, and an odd mixture of confusion and delight has him arching an eyebrow at me. His gaze bounces between the book I'm barely holding back and the minuscule space between us, but he doesn't step back. The longer we stand like this, the more insistent the book becomes, lurching against my fingertips.

"Do you need some help?" An amused chuckle shadows his question, and I wonder if he notices the way the air around us is once again prickling.

He starts to reach up in an attempt to help and a wordless squeak escapes me.

Oliver pauses, perplexed, and then slowly lowers his hand once again. "Or not?"

I giggle nervously again, trying not to show how much I'm struggling to fight the adamant book. It's so high that I struggle to hold it in place with my fingertips, and my wrist is starting to ache.

"I don't know if Don mentioned it, but we also have a coffee bar." The words come out in a rush of breath that does little to hide the goose bumps that start to pepper my skin.

"Oh?" He smirks as if I've invited him on a date.

I'd be pleased by his apparent interest if I weren't so preoccupied with the murderous romance novel I'm fighting. I've spent the last few years so focused on Grandma and Moonlit Pages that a love life hasn't even been on the table. Not that it was going that great before. Right now, though, I have bigger problems at hand.

"Uh-huh, it's run by my friend. Lucy!" I yell her name, my voice cracking around the letters in a desperate plea, trying to sound casual and failing.

Lucy's head pops out from around the end of the aisle, and her keen eyes are quick to assess the situation.

"Yeah, boss?"

"Oliver, Lucy. Lucy, this is the new bakery owner, Oliver." I race through introductions, gritting my teeth into a pained smile. My shoulders and triceps are burning, and along with everything else running through my head, I make a mental note to spend more time at the gym. I would totally be the first to die in whatever fantasy world Oliver stepped out of if I can't even fight back a 300-page paperback. "Could you treat him to one of your signature drinks? Please?"

Without a moment's hesitation, Lucy jumps into action, taking the hint.

"Of course!" She coos, threading an arm through the elbow Oliver didn't offer and guiding him away. "So nice to meet you. Quick question: will you be selling apple fritters?"

"Uh . . ." Oliver glances back at me one last time as if he's still trying to figure out what just happened. For a brief moment, I'm swept away in his steely gaze, almost forgetting to fight the insistent book at my fingertips. But in the next heartbeat, he's turning his attention to the whirlwind on his arm. "Of course. It would be a pretty depressing bakery without them."

Lucy gives him an approving nod. "Oh, good, we can be friends."

I sigh with relief when the two turn the corner and let the book launch itself off the shelf. I manage to catch it before it crashes to the floor, and I fall back against the shelving unit, shaking the ache out of my arm. At least my hand-eye coordination isn't too bad.

I give myself one heavy breath to collect myself before turning to reshelve the naughty books in my arms.

"Of all days, you two choose today to be difficult," I scold them under my breath.

"You." I study the pink cover of the first, with illustrated flowers surrounding the title, *Meet Cutes and Mischief.* "Calm down and stay in your place." I slide it back into its spot.

I eye the cover of the second one. Where the first one looked like it could have been a cozy romantic comedy, this one screams dark romance. Hands wrap around a throat dripping with bloodred jewels, set against a dark background. The title, *Beyond a Shadowed Heart,* is written in curling white letters that end in razor-sharp points.

"And you . . . I think I'll take you to the back."

Chapter Three

The streets of Ashwood Haven come alive as night descends. Twinkling lights in all shades of orange, purple, and green are strung all over Main Street, wrapped around trees, iron lamp-posts, and colorful awnings. Their inviting glow reflects off brightly lit storefront windows, all the downtown businesses embracing the late-night influx of shoppers eager to revel in tonight's festivities.

I, on the other hand, can do nothing but pace back and forth before the stairs leading up to a stage smack dab in the center of town. Or, as I've been referring to it in my head, the execution block built for no other purpose than my eternal humiliation.

"Are you ready, Amelia?"

I jump at the offhanded question, too busy tapping my note-cards against my palm to notice Stacy's approach. "Hm?"

She ticks something off on her clipboard with every new thing she sees before her appraising eyes flick to me. My anxiety must be written across my face because her head snaps up, her metal clipboard lowering a couple of inches.

"Are you ready?" Stacy nods with each word, a light panic emphasizing each syllable.

I pluck at the corner of my notecards with a nail, the cards already creased and worn from my anxious fiddling over the last half hour.

"Yeah, I'm good. I'm ready." The words come out in a breathy huff, and I'm not sure whom I'm trying to reassure more, me or her.

With a heavy sigh, Stacy lets the clipboard hang by her side as she reaches out and rests a hand on my shoulder. "You'll do fine. Tonight's super easy. Want to run through it again?"

I nearly give myself whiplash nodding so hard, unable to keep from swaying on my feet; my skirt brushes against my knees with each movement. Behind her, the crowd is already thickening, people packing in tight before the stage. Soon, I won't even be able to pick out the other side of Main Street unless I climb the stairs of doom.

"So, all you have to do is wait for my signal, then you'll go up and announce the parade, which is when I'll radio down to Luke to start. Once the parade is over, you'll give a close-out speech and declare the kick-off to the festival. That's it." She dips down, trying to catch my eye and assure herself that I'm not about to screw up all her meticulous planning. "Okay?"

This time, my nod is small and hesitant, but with one last deep breath, I shake off the last of my jitters and paint on my sunniest smile. "Okay, yes. I can do this. No problem."

Stacy eyes me, utterly unconvinced by my poor performance,

and opens her mouth to say more when the radio hanging on her belt chirps.

Luke's staticky voice comes through the speaker. "We're ready on this end. On your go."

The coordinator (or, as Lucy refers to her, my wrangler) jumps into action, double-checking her intricate stack of lists and tables on her clipboard before holding the radio to her mouth.

"Sounds good. Hold until my signal." Stacy returns her attention to me, my previous doubts forgotten as she ushers me toward the stage steps. "This is it. You're going to do great!"

I stumble up the first step, as if my feet are in cahoots with my clenching stomach, trying to keep me safe on the ground. With one last deep breath, I put all my focus into putting one foot in front of the other, ignoring the weight of hundreds of eyes settling upon me as I climb higher. I swallow hard and glance at one of the local bands lined up, ready to go. Their respective guitars and drumsticks anxiously wait to give background music to the coming parade as soon as I do my thing. They all offer me encouraging smiles, but all I notice is how the world around me grows quiet as the crowd falls silent with anticipation.

The journey to the center of the stage feels like the longest of my life, the microphone stand acting as my finish line. In an attempt to pretend I'm anywhere but here, I think back to the last book I finished. During the finale of an epic fantasy series, the heroine spent day after day trudging across harsh landscapes and faced unimaginable evil. I imagine I'm walking beside her, because somehow the prospect of facing a brooding dragon is far less terrifying than the very real possibility of tripping or becoming sick in front of all these people.

When I finally make it to my destination—my proverbial

mountain top on this imaginary quest—I am harshly flung back into reality as I look out over the crowd. I can only glance over them before I have to turn my focus to my notecards, clutched between white-knuckled fingers. Between my racing heart and trembling grip, I can't even read my own handwriting, and I try to recall the words via memory from the dozen or so times I practiced the speech.

But when I open my mouth, my throat goes dry and the words have utterly vanished. I swallow hard and smile, doing my best to straighten my shoulders and focus on the storefronts across the way, but my lips start to tremble with the force of holding them upright.

"Good evening, everyone." My voice cracks around the words, and I have to clear my throat before I can go on. "Welcome to the kick-off of Ashwood Haven's legendary Halloween festival. My name is Amelia, I'm the owner of Moonlit Pages, and I am this year's festival host and sponsor. I can't wait to spend the next week with you all carving pumpkins, watching Halloween movies, and judging costume contests. But first, please turn your attention to Main Street and enjoy our opening night parade." Despite it not being the speech I wrote out and rehearsed, cheering ensues, giving me a chance to breathe before the band erupts behind me, and everyone turns away, my presence immediately forgotten. They play a cover of some upbeat pop song, but the music fades beneath the roaring blood in my ears.

The masses migrate to the sidewalks of Main Street, packing in tight for a chance to witness the first night of Halloween.

Knees shaking, I hurry off the stage in time to hear Stacy radio Luke to start the parade, and I sigh with relief. It had been a fraction of what I planned to say, but at least it's over. All I have to do now is watch the parade and give the closing speech.

My palms start sweating at the thought, and I try not to think about it.

"See? Easy peasy." Stacy starts ushering me toward Main Street like a kindergarten teacher herding a frantic child, not bothering to glance at me as she studies the surrounding area for some minute detail. "We have a prime spot set up for you to watch the parade, and then I'll come get you when it's time for the closing speech."

Mindlessly, I follow where she leads me until I'm settled in a reserved spot on the street curb. It's not until she races away to deal with who-knows-what that I take my first easy breath of the night. I'm not necessarily alone, surrounded by parade watchers, but no one is paying attention to me and I can exist in my own little bubble for a while. I sigh through my nose and let my jitters run free, shaking out my shoulders as if that will get rid of the lingering feeling of so many eyes on me.

From down the street, a float covered in glittering strands of orange and purple turns the corner and starts crawling its way down the main artery of town. I can hardly hear anything over the cheering crowd, people clapping as the float rolls closer.

Closing my eyes, I drown out the people as if they are white noise in the background and toe the corner of the curb. Despite my efforts, I end up dwelling on all the words I intended to say and forgot.

Grandma would have done it better. She would have strutted across that stage as if it had been constructed just for her, and, magic or no, she would have charmed everyone into thinking she ran the town single-handedly. Not only would she have given a better speech, but she wouldn't have needed notes to do it. She would have gotten up there and spoken from the heart about town tradition and the long lines of families that have spent more generations than they can document right here in Ashwood Haven. She would have . . .

A familiar deep voice breaks through my inner downward spiral, close enough that his breath brushes against my ear. "You did great."

Startled, I turn to find Oliver standing behind my shoulder and wonder how he got so close without me noticing. I definitely would have noticed him if he'd been here when Stacy brought me over. He's a head taller than anyone else in the crowd near us; his broad shoulders shrouded in a dark peacoat, blocking the view of several people. Even if I hadn't seen him initially, I would have felt him and the way the air buzzes with frantic energy between us.

I scan the faces around us, searching for upset patrons to give an apologetic look to, but I come up short. People have had these spots claimed all day to get the best view of the parade. Yet, here he is, standing with the toes of his shoes right on the edge of the sidewalk, and not a single person seems bothered—as if he materialized out of nowhere.

I swallow and automatically start rubbing the hem of my sweater between my fingers, the yarn rolling back and forth, hidden beneath the sleeve of my jacket.

"Thank you," I choke out, doing my best to sound polite and trying not to stare at those steel blue eyes. "I'm glad to see you got a good spot. The parade is a crowd favorite."

I turn my attention back to the street, the first float finally crawling by.

It's tiered, like a wedding cake, with Don standing at the very top dressed as a circus ringmaster. On each of the other tiers are dancers and gymnasts performing various routines and stunts that garner whoops and hollers from the onlookers. Don makes a show of the whole thing, soaking in every drop of attention he's getting. He gestures with his top hat and cane, pointing to the most impressive act of the moment and giving all the performers outrageous names.

"I am curious why you gave the speech instead of Don. He's the one who welcomed me to town; it seems like something he would do."

Oliver's words brush against my neck, and when I look back over my shoulder, I expect him to be looming close, too close. Only, I find him keeping as respectful of a distance as he can in such a crowded area. From here, I shouldn't be able to hear such quiet words, and yet, the ghost of his breath lingers, heating my cheeks.

I dip my chin to hide the creeping blush, chalking up the goose bumps rising along my arms to the cool night air, despite my coat. "I'm the festival sponsor and host."

Oliver tips his head to the side in thought. "What does that mean exactly?"

I clear my throat, trying to focus more on the upcoming float where little ballerinas bounce around in witches' costumes on broomsticks than on the man whose voice seems to be caressing my ear. "Every year, one of the businesses in town sponsors the festival. They help coordinate events, fund prizes, and choose a person, usually the owner, to act as host. It rotates. This year it's Moonlit Pages's turn, and in a few years, it will be your turn."

I glance up at the burly man towering over me, and a smirk pulls at the corner of his lip, revealing that dimple that makes my heart flutter. "Trust me, no one wants to hear me try and give a speech."

"I'm sure you'll do fine," I reply, the words sticking to my tongue as his eyes study mine. It's a kind and polite reassurance that has no right feeling as intimate as it does. The crowd around me melts away, turning to nothing but a drone in the background, and I'm suddenly very aware of what that achingly familiar feeling is that's been building between us.

The magic steeped into every crack and crevice of Ashwood Haven crackles across my skin, pulling at something deep in my chest and knocking the breath from my lungs.

As if my eyes know exactly where to go, my attention is drawn back to the parade. The little ballerinas have gone from barely coordinated dancing to . . . flying. With each little skip and hop on their broomsticks, they hover a little longer, until one of them lingers too long and the jump turns into a hover. In a single skip, she's leaped nearly five feet, hanging in the air like a cartoon character.

My heart leaps up through my throat as the dance teacher watches the already tenuous focus of the group completely dissolve. One by one, each ballerina notices they can suddenly hop further than a kangaroo and, like any child would, start to test their limits. Quickly, the dance routine turns into an all-out contest to see who can get the highest.

Before I can think through the decision, I dart into the street, beelining for the dancers-turned-birds because not only do I recognize those brooms, I supplied them. They're from *my* shop. They are always a best seller in our toy section: Charmed broomsticks that make the kids' hops go a little further for a bit more fun. But now, that innocent charm seems to have grown into a full-on flying spell that has one little girl floating three feet off the ground.

Spectators lining the sidewalk start to notice the flying ballerinas, and their excited chatter turns to worried whispers. Several people rush into the street, pulling giggling witches from their broomsticks. Quicker than a rumor spreads through a small town, the whispers become a roar of gasps and cries.

Sprinting as fast as I can, I reach the highest girl and pull her from the hovering broom, expecting it to fall back to the ground with a clatter the way it's supposed to once it's lost its rider. Instead, it stays put midair, as if it's been hung by a string from the stars above.

Mind spinning, I do the only thing I can think of in a moment of panic and stutter through the incantation backward. It takes more tries than I care to admit, but finally the broom falls to the bricks with a crash.

"Stop! Girls! Feet on the ground!" the dance teacher shrieks, racing around, trying to control all the little jumping beans.

Before I can celebrate my little victory, I spot another ballerina starting to spin like a tornado down the street. Her black and purple witch's hat goes flying into the crowd, her blonde hair whipping in circles as she screeches with delight.

Adrenaline pumping, the concerned shouts of onlookers get drowned out by the sound of my pounding heart. I race after her, willing her to hold on tight as I try to catch her before she can crash into a vintage trash truck hauling pumpkins. With each passing second, though, I realize my chances of reaching her in time dwindle. She's spinning too fast, and my legs don't move quickly enough. The best I can hope for is to catch the whirling witch before she hits the street.

Moments from colliding with the truck bed at the velocity of a washing machine, Oliver swoops in like the love interest of a cheesy rom-com. With a heartbeat to spare, he snatches the girl off the spinning broom and into the safety of his arms.

"I got ya!" He balances her in his arms, draped over his forearm like a towel on a clothes line, before setting her gently on her feet. The words to the inverted incantation are on the tip of my tongue when the broom clatters to the ground all on its own.

Instead, I pull Sophie into my arms. "Oh, thank goodness, you're alright!" I cry, cupping her cheeks in my palms so I can verify with my own eyes that she's unharmed.

Sophie only giggles conspiratorially, not a hint of fear to be found. "Miss Amelia, did you see me? I can fly!"

"Maybe keep your feet on the ground for a little while. Okay, kid?" Oliver suggests, patting her on the head once.

I pull the ballerina into a bone-crushing hug, not only relieved that she's safe but that her fathers, Mike and Jim, aren't going to kill me. They spent years going through the adoption process, and I'd be incurring the *entire* town's wrath if Sophie had so much as scraped her left elbow.

I'm about to thank Oliver for his heroism when a scream echoes from behind me. Before I even have a chance to turn and see what it is now, Oliver takes off toward the new source of chaos, coat flapping behind him.

I'm horrified to find that as I sprint after him, a skeleton on one of the floats is dancing all on its own. The boy who's supposed to be operating it like a puppet cries out as the plastic skeleton does the jig, its knobby knees flailing back and forth in the jerkiest dance I've ever seen. Then, another starts dancing until all four are wiggling about independently from the teenagers who should be controlling them.

As I'm racing down the street, I realize I recognize these props too! They're the faux skeletons I found in the bookstore basement while searching for decorations. Grandma used to hang them out front. They would rattle in the breeze, but them being charmed was news to me, and they certainly weren't supposed to do *that*.

Just as Oliver reaches the float, Lucy comes flying out of Moonlit Pages and shoulders her way through the stunned crowd. I meet her at the corner of the float, and she shoves a bag of moon-soaked salt into my hands before helping me onto the platform.

This time, I have no idea what spell Grandma used, and my chances of guessing it backward are slim to none. Instead, I grab a handful of salt, throw it at the dancing skeleton, and recite a general reversal spell, hoping for the best. The decoration freezes, its unhinged jaw clacking open and closed before collapsing into a heap of plastic.

I start toward the next one, but it's already in a mercifully still pile at Oliver's feet. Before I can question how he managed to do it, another teenager shrieks. A discoing skeleton is closing in on where she's backed up against the center tier of the float. I repeat the same process I did with the first, and thankfully, it falls into a heap of motionless fake bones.

Oliver shoves the fourth and final skeleton off the edge of the float, and it shatters into a dozen pieces of wiggling plastic. I upend my bag of salt, dumping it atop the bone pile, whisper my reversal spell, and the pieces finally lie still.

The whole parade comes to a standstill, and the crowd goes quiet for several long-drawn-out seconds.

Panic starts to rise in my throat as I meet the wide eyes and slack jaws of onlookers openly staring at me atop a float. I do my best to straighten my spine and smile back at them, but my lips shake beneath the weight of their stares. All I can imagine is one tourist shouting *witch* and Ashwood Haven reverting to Puritan-era Salem to reenact witch trials with Lucy and I standing side by side at the chopping block.

Well . . . at least I'll have an aesthetic death, with the town all decorated. Maybe they'll do it on one of the floats.

Yeah, that would be fitting . . .

Cheers erupt from every corner of the street; even the tormented teenagers and terrified dance teacher start laughing.

I'm utterly stunned.

It's not until Oliver grabs my hand and makes a grand gesture that I realize they all think I staged the whole thing as an elaborate prank. I glance down at Lucy, looking for some sort of direction on what I should do, but her eyes are wide with questions. I shrug and shake my head, letting her know I'm just as confused as she is.

I start toward the edge of the float to jump down, but before I have the chance, the whole thing lurches forward. The moving floor sends me off-balance. I reach out to balance myself against Oliver, but he's no longer by my side—he's already on the street below. He throws me an apologetic smile, maybe for abandoning me, before melting into the crowd, leaving me behind to face the world on my own.

One of the teenagers appears at my side, laughing and waving. She beams with the thrill of being the center of attention, and I do my best to play off her endless energy.

Together, we ride the float all the way to the end of the parade.

When the float finally turns out of sight of Main Street and comes to a stop, the teenage girl with a cloud of coiled black hair bounces on her toes. "That was so cool! How did you do it?"

My cheeks ache from all the smiling, and I have to work my jaw before answering her. "Do what?"

She rolls her big brown eyes in the dramatic way only teenagers can. "The skeletons and brooms, obviously. How did you do it without anyone knowing?"

My mouth falls open, but no words come out. I have absolutely no idea what to tell her, and I realize I'm about to be bombarded with about a hundred more questions just like this. Specifically, from outraged parents of flying ballerinas and a festival coordinator who had her entire schedule thrown off.

Mercifully, Lucy's voice cuts through my thoughts and the ever-growing awkward silence, saving me from a bumbling explanation.

"Nope. No revealing your secrets!" A mess of red hair appears at the base of the float and holds out a hand to help me down.

I give the teenage girl an apologetic smile, much like the one Oliver gave me, and force myself not to sag with relief. The moment my feet hit the ground, Lucy throws an arm over my shoulders and leads me away.

"What the hell was that?" she whispers frantically.

I shake my head. "I don't know."

"But wasn't that the stuff you donated? And did you feel whatever happened with the magic?"

I nod, opening my mouth to answer, but she's already off on another ramble of questions.

"And what was up with that Oliver guy? What was he doing?"

I grab Lucy by the shoulders, stopping her in her tracks. "I don't know! I don't know what happened. I don't know what he was doing. I have no idea what's going on. The books earlier and now this?"

"Well, you better figure it out pretty damn quick," Lucy whisper-yells back, her voice rising to a pitch that is so unlike her it sends a thread of panic through my heart.

"Amelia!" Stacy shouts behind me.

My spine goes ramrod straight, and I exchange an alarmed look with Lucy before smoothing my face into a pleasant expression and turning on my heel.

"Amelia, there you are." The coordinator breathes a sigh of relief at the sight of me before ushering me back toward the town square and away from Lucy. "Your little side quest threw everything off. I need to get you back to the stage so you can be ready when the parade ends. Oh, and we're going to have to discuss that stunt you pulled. I appreciate a good prank as much as the next person, but we're aiming for organized fun here. I need you to check in with me first before you do anything else like that, so I can ensure it fits into the schedule."

I absently nod to her rambling, only half listening since I definitely don't have any other surprises up my sleeve.

Stacy leads me to the back side of the stage. Like a babysitter wrangling a toddler, she gives me a place to stand and tells me not to leave my little box. The panicked coordinator takes off, triple- and quadruple-checking her clipboard as she chatters into her radio.

I shift on my feet, my mind reeling, when I catch sight of a large figure leaning against a tree at the far end of the square. Oliver gives me a small wave, and even from this distance, I spot a twinkle in his steely eyes and a mischievous curve to his lips.

I watch him for a moment, considering marching right over and demanding he explain himself and the role he played in what just happened, but I realize that doing so would invite questions for which I also have no answers.

So, instead, I give him an appreciative nod back and mouth the words, "Thank you."

Whether he played a part in this or not, he did help get it all under control, and for that, I'm grateful.

"Okay, Amelia, you're up. Let's go!" Stacy shouts at me from the stairs.

I hurry toward her, throwing one last glance over my shoulder, but Oliver has vanished.

The space beneath the looming oak tree is conspicuously empty, leaving nothing but the swaying branches and the autumn leaves dancing beneath the glow of the street lights.

Chapter Four

"Flying ballerinas!" Lucy shrieks, throwing her hands up in disbelief from where she sits on the edge of a display table, one leg tucked up beneath her. "I just can't believe it."

I sigh, grabbing a stack of thrillers and fitting them into their slots on the shelf one at a time. "I know. Want to know how? Because you keep repeating it."

"I keep repeating it because it's so unbelievable. I get the skeletons; Grandma loved her pranks. I can just picture her giggling as she set that charm, poised to go wrong the moment the decorations left the store grounds. But *flying ballerinas*?" Lucy grabs one of the little skeletons sitting on the table and flies it through the air as if to make her point.

"I don't know what happened!" I wave one of the paperbacks at her, the pages flapping and flopping. "I charmed those brooms myself. The same charm we use every. Single. Year. That never should have happened."

Lucy chews on the inside of her cheek, studying me with black-lined green eyes while toying with the skeleton figurine's flexible joints. "Are you sick?"

I pause, tipping my head at her. "No."

"Maybe you said it wrong," she offers, pointing at me with one of the toy's hands.

"I didn't say it wrong, Lucy! I read it from the freaking book." I throw out a hand, gesturing toward the coffee bar. From here, I can just make out the corner of the spell book passed through generations of my family, so old it would be nothing but dust if it weren't for the incantation keeping it together. *The* book that holds every spell, charm, incantation, and hex my family has ever used, developed, or (admittedly) stolen with every new generation of witches.

Lucy worries at her lip, contemplating every possible option as I shelve another stack of books. "Has anything changed? Was anything different at the parade?"

Pressing my lips together, I stare at the colorful spines, studying the rainbow of colors and font styles. Blues, greens, and blacks are all lined up nicely on the shelf in neat rows, decorated with jagged titles meant to instill fear and intrigue. Mentally, I run through all the events from the night before, both planned and unplanned.

"I mean . . ." My shoulders sag. "I was pretty worked up about the speeches." I scowl at the books, the admittance burning my tongue.

Lucy shrugs, barely acknowledging my show of weakness as she continues to make her skeleton dance on her thigh in an imitation of the ones last night. "Perfectly understandable. Everyone hates public speaking."

"Grandma didn't," I whisper, letting my forehead thump against the books.

Lucy rests the toy in her lap, expression softening. "You're not Grandma, Amelia," she says quietly, letting the reminder hang heavy between us before straightening and continuing in a far more confident voice. "Besides, Grandma wasn't so perfect." She waggles her arms. "Hello? Dancing skeletons?"

I half-sob, half-laugh at her imitation of last night's disastrous decorations. "Luce, what am I going to do?"

"Well, you certainly can't keep hosting if your anxiety is going to cause the magic to run amok through the town."

"I don't have anxiety," I retort.

Lucy raises a scolding eyebrow at me.

"Fine," I sigh. I fall back against the bookcase, clutching a novel to my chest as if it can shield me from reality. "So, what? Turn the whole thing over to Don? I can't do that."

Lucy snorts, the corner of her lip lifting. "Why not? I would. He'd be thrilled. He never gets to host."

I shake my head, unwilling to even contemplate the option. "No way. I can't have the whole town thinking I can't handle things now that Grandma is gone. Besides, I'm not even sure that's what it was. My *anxiety* was worse before I got on stage, not after."

Lucy gives me a sad, tight-lipped smile, a mix of understanding and pity shadowing her eyes.

"Ugh, stop looking at me like that."

She throws her hands up in surrender, toy skeleton rattling. "Fine, fine. So, we need to figure out what else could have caused the magic to flip out and find a solution before the market tonight. That can't be too hard, right? Run me through everything that happened again."

"I gave the speech, and then Stacy brought me to the host's

section. The first float came by with Don and the gymnasts doing their thing, and I was talking to Oliver, and then—"

"Wait"—Lucy holds up a hand to cut me off—"you were talking to the new guy in town when the ballerinas started flying?"

"Would you stop saying that?"

"Would you answer the question?"

I sigh and wave my book at her. "Fine, yes. I was talking to Oliver when the brooms started acting up."

She nods thoughtfully, looking like she's working through a math problem involving a guy who bought eighty-seven bottles of soda with a buy-three-get-one-free coupon. "And then what?"

"Then I ran over to do a charm reversal, and he helped gather up one of the girls—"

"Wait!"

I glare at her for cutting me off again, but she doesn't seem to notice.

"The new guy was helping with the flying ballerinas? You left that part out last time."

"Maybe you didn't hear me because you were so focused on the *flying ballerinas.*" I raise an eyebrow and challenge her with a tip of my head.

"Point taken, I won't say it anymore. Please tell me how the new guy helped with your unruly sticks."

I narrow my eyes at her. "That is *not* an improvement."

She waves her hands at me, urging me to continue.

I roll my eyes until the back of my head hits the hardbacks behind me. "Yes, we were talking, and then the brooms started acting up. Sophie started spiraling toward the pumpkin truck, and he ran over and got it under control before I could get there."

"I thought you said the brooms needed a reversal charm?"

I nod, thinking back to how the broom kept hovering even though the charm should have only worked with a rider present, not after. "They did. That's what made the whole thing even weirder. It's like they had a mind of their own. Like something amplified the magic, or it was fighting back, or something."

"So, if the brooms required a reversal, how did Oliver get it under control before you got there?"

"Well, he . . ." I think back to that moment, playing it over in my mind. I watch Oliver swoop in out of nowhere and rescue the little ballerina from her broom. I'd been so caught up in Sophie's safety, the discoing skeletons, and screaming teenagers that I didn't take a second to question how the broom stopped flying. "I don't know."

"And he helped with the skeletons, too, right? He was already on the float when I arrived."

Brows furrowing, I remember one of the skeletons lying in a lifeless heap at his feet before I'd even gotten the moon-soaked salt from Lucy. "Yeah, he did."

Lucy jumps to her feet, forgetting her toy on the table, and I follow close on her heels as she saunters toward the front of the store. She leans against the frame of the bay window overlooking Main Street, crossing her arms with a smirk. I follow her gaze to the bakery storefront across the way, where a banner hangs, proclaiming: **Grand Opening Friday!**

Through the windows, I watch Oliver walk through the bakery, wiping down tables. His white T-shirt hugs his brawny frame, and the sleeves wrap around his thick arms as he flips another chair over, situating it around one of the small white tables left behind by Miss Laura's retirement.

"What are you thinking?" I ask her, reading the gleam behind those devious eyes.

"I'm thinking the new guy might know more about what's going on than he's letting on." Lucy waggles her eyebrows at me. "And I think it's up to *you*, as sponsor, to figure out what it is."

"Me?" I squeal, indignant. "I've already planned everything, and I'm hosting. Why don't *you* figure out what it is?"

"Because I'm not the one who was flirting with him at the parade last night."

"We were not flirting. We were just . . . talking."

Lucy dismisses me with a wave of her hand. "Psh. As sponsor and host, I think it's up to you to ensure the new guy gets a good tour of . . . What event is tonight?"

I cock my hip and give her my best exasperated glare. "The market—which you very well know."

"Ah, yes. The Witch's Market. The perfect place to show someone around, introduce them to the town, pry into their personal life . . ." Her mischievous grin is so wide that even her eyes sparkle.

I worry at my lip and narrow my eyes at her, trying to think of any way out of this. "And if he doesn't go to the market tonight?"

"Oh, we certainly can't have that. You'll have to go over and invite him."

I roll my eyes and push a sigh through my nose. She isn't going to let up; it isn't the Lucy way. "Fine, but you have to keep the coffee bar open late tonight like you promised. You can't just pretend you have no idea how to make a latte after five."

"Deal!" she chirps before turning away and heading for the espresso maker. "Don't forget to ask about the fritters."

I scowl at her retreating back, and I push through the front door before I can talk myself out of it. The bell overhead happily announces my exit.

Despite the cool autumn day, shoppers and tourists crowd the sidewalks, studying the seasonally decorated storefronts beneath turning leaves and unlit lampposts that will give Main Street a mythical glow come sundown. I hurry across the street, pulling the sleeves of my sweater down over my hands when a brisk gust of wind bites through the weave. It lifts not only my dark hair and hem of my skirt, but the fallen leaves that scatter across the brick road with a hiss too.

Pausing before the glass bakery door, I search for Oliver in the shadows. Instinctively, my fingers find the cuff of my sweater, worrying at the strands with every passing second. When I don't find him, I lift my hand to knock on the wooden frame, and pause, rethinking everything in my life that's led to this moment.

Since when did I become this girl? The one who boldly invites the new man in town out on a date when we're barely on a first-name basis. Something urges me on, like a rope tied around my waist pulling me in, and I remind myself that this is for the good of the town. Our festivals and holiday celebrations are what bring people to our little corner of the world, and if our biggest event of the year goes south, it could risk more than just my pride.

So, I suck it up and knock my knuckles against the door, rattling the seasonal wreath hanging on it.

A burly form pops out from the backroom, and Oliver smiles at me from behind the counter, making my heart flutter.

I motion for him to unlock the door, trying to ignore how his T-shirt strains against his broad shoulders or how large his hands are as he wipes them off with a towel.

He smirks at me through the crack in the door, leaning against the frame with his forearm. "I don't have any apple fritters yet."

I chuckle. "No, it's not that, though Lucy told me to ask about those. Actually"—I shiver, hugging myself against the cold—"do you mind if I come in? It's a little brisk out."

"Oh, of course." He stands back, waving me inside before closing the door with a clatter.

The bakery is exactly as I remember. The floor shines with polished black and white tiles beneath an array of tables, their white paint chipped with age and wear. The bench seat against the far wall is still piled high with cushions and pillows, the same deep green they've always been. For some reason, the familiarity shocks me. I realize that part of me expected it to be completely different now that it's under new ownership for the first time in my life, even though I was here weeks ago.

Miss Laura owned this bakery for nearly her entire life, having purchased it from the family that originally opened it. Looking around, I'm flooded with a warm wave of nostalgia as sweet as the sugar cookies she used to sell. I can clearly picture Lucy and me huddled in the corner every Wednesday afternoon after school, claiming to do homework while we devoured croissants. The phantom taste of cocoa and sugar coats my tongue at the memory of all the times Grandma brought me here after a breakup, telling me that brownies were the best way to heal a broken heart.

"Are you okay?" Oliver asks gently, a soft hand on my elbow.

I swallow hard, willing away the fresh line of tears that's appeared on my lashes at the thought of Grandma, and turn to him, a small smile tugging at the corner of my lip. "Yes, of course. I'm fine."

He studies me for a moment before giving me a slow nod, as if he's seeing right past my hostess mask. "Right. So, what can I do for you?"

"Well, with you being new to town and me being this year's host of the legendary Ashwood Haven Halloween festival, I wanted to offer you the *exclusive* chance to be my personal guest at the Witch's Market tonight." I bounce as I talk, giving everything an extra layer of exaggeration and jazz hands in the hopes that I come off more good-natured and less nervous.

He chuckles. "Exclusive, you say?"

"Oh yes, playing host has many perks I'd happily share."

"Such as?"

I tap my chin with a single finger and purse my lips in thought. "Well, unlimited hot chocolate and first dibs on all the good booths for starters."

"I didn't know witches had hot chocolate," he teases, his eyes sparkling with amusement.

Golden-brown waves bounce, and his shoulders shake, the sound of his soft chuckles making my breath catch. His laugh is warm and inviting, causing my stomach to flip in a way I haven't felt in a long time.

The corner of my mouth lifts, genuine this time, as I meet his lively gaze. Something about the moment reminds me of a scene from the romantic fantasy I read yesterday between customers. The bold and flirty main character was always ready to say and do whatever it took to get her way. Of course, if flirting didn't work, she happily turned to a more . . . vicious form of persuasion, usually involving some form of sharp blade. I channel her nonetheless (the less violent side of her, anyway).

"I bet I could teach you a lot of things about witches."

Embarrassment immediately wraps itself around my stomach, and I clamp my lips together to keep from taking the words back.

But Oliver takes a small step closer, the dimple in his cheek deepening. "Well, I'm nothing if not eager to learn."

He's so close I could easily reach out and run a hand over the veins in his arms, heat rolling off him. It makes me want to step into his arms and fold his presence around me like a blanket. Those wintery eyes pin me in place, and I have to stop myself from squirming.

It's an odd sensation that makes me take a step back instead.

"Then I'll see you tonight?" The question comes out breathier than I intended, my bravado melting away.

"It's a date," he agrees.

Chapter Five

Dry leaves crunch beneath the heel of my boots as I sway on my feet, pushing my hands deeper into my pockets and admiring the arch made of plastic pumpkins and balloons of various spooky colors towering above me. I wait for Oliver, swathed in the glow of string lights and lampposts. Tourists and festivalgoers flow past me and into the market, chattering in tightly packed groups about what treats they might find and the "spells" they plan to buy.

Customers flow in and out of brightly lit storefronts as if it were a Saturday afternoon, bags hanging off their elbows before they've even made it to the booths behind me. Two girls bundled in cute coats and scarves come giggling out of Moonlit Pages, steaming lattes in hand as they walk arm-in-arm toward the market. They smile at me as they pass, a spark of recognition in their eyes.

Moments later, Oliver steps out of his new bakery, his charcoal peacoat hugging his frame as he locks the door behind him.

I bounce on my toes when he spots me beneath the arch, resisting the urge to run right up to his side.

"Have you lot ever considered celebrating a warmer holiday?" His shoulders jump up to his ears in an exaggerated shiver.

I shrug and weave an arm through his, pulling him through the entrance and deeper into the market. "You can't have a Witch's Market on National Donut Day."

He snorts. "Can't argue with that logic. What is a Witch's Market anyway?" Oliver eyes the passing stalls closely, craning his neck to get a better look at an elaborately carved chess set.

I lead him through the booths and guide him toward one enveloped in shades of sparkling blue and iridescent purples. The table is laden with an array of candles with names like *Love Potion* and *Calming Essence.*

"It's a normal market, but Halloween-themed. Don't worry, I won't let anyone curse you or sell you a bad spell," I tease, knowing full well that I'm one of only two people in this town actually capable of hexing him.

He picks up one of the candles, studying the scrolling label that reads *Abundance.* "That is greatly appreciated," he mutters before unscrewing the top and taking a big whiff before I can stop him.

Instead, I bite my lip, waiting for the reaction I know is coming.

Oliver's face screws up, and he recoils, holding the candle at bay like a kitten trying to scratch his eyes out. "Oh my . . ." He coughs into his elbow, eyes starting to water, and I can't contain my laugh. "What *is* that?"

"It's the scent of abundance," I chuckle, failing to hide my amusement and knowing full well it smells like a cross between the sweetest cupcake in the world and a sweaty bodybuilder straight from the gym. He gives me a skeptical look that I catch out of the corner of my eye before screwing the top back on.

"The abundance of what? Dirty socks soaked in buttercream?"

A genuine smile pulls at my lips at how accurate that descriptor is, my shoulders shaking with laughter as I grab one labeled *Sunrise*. I unscrew the top and hold it out to him.

"Here," I offer, swallowing my giggles, "try this one."

His eyes flit between me and the candle, debating whether or not to trust me after I let him sniff *Abundance*. I shake the jar at him, and reluctantly, he leans in and gives it a hesitant whiff. Instantly, his face lights up, and he takes another deeper sniff, drinking in the scent of oranges, ginger, and cinnamon.

"Oh, that's much better. I can't say I've ever sniffed the sunrise, but I'll take that over *Abundance* any day." He rubs his nose as if trying to rid it of the memory.

I laugh again, feeling lighter than I have in months. I take a deep, easy breath just as the booth owner notices us standing by the table.

"Hey, Amelia! Find anything you like?" Thomas asks, rubbing his hands together and beaming at me, his rosy pink cheeks reflecting the low lights of the market.

"Oh, I'm only browsing tonight. Though I think Oliver here could use something to help with his grand opening."

"Grand opening? You must be the young man who bought Laura's bakery." Thomas reaches out across the table to shake Oliver's hand, smiling from ear to ear. "I'm Thomas, nice to meet you. Ya know, I saw you checking out *Abundance*. That's a great one to have as a new business owner."

Oliver does his best to hide his grimace, and I have to cough into my sleeve to hide my snort.

"Actually . . ." He scans the table and plucks the closest jar of *Sunrise* he can find. "I think I'm more of a morning person. I'll take this one."

"Another excellent choice!" Thomas booms, gleaming with pride at making a sale. As the town's resident carpenter, Thomas's candle making is nothing more than a passion hobby that he pulls out a few times a year. Everyone in town knows that each new scent will either be amazing or the most vile thing one has ever smelled—with no in between. But watching him puff up with a childlike glee every time he sells one makes it worth it every time.

Thomas leaves to wrap up the candle, and I burst out laughing, covering my mouth with a hand.

"Thanks for the help," Oliver teases, elbowing my shoulder. I'm laughing so hard that I trip over my own feet and throw my head back.

"You didn't actually have to buy anything," I say between chuckles.

"Tell that to Thomas," he whispers between clenched teeth, jerking his head in the direction of the candlemaker, but he can't hide the grin pulling at his lips.

Once we've secured Oliver's purchase, I pull him away and introduce him to every business owner in town with a booth. He buys something every few stalls, and by the time we're halfway through, he has a bag on his arm bulging with a crocheted hat, oven mitts covered in moons and stars, a salsa mix, and various other goodies.

"You don't have to buy something from everyone to make them like you."

Oliver shrugs, holding out the bag and letting it dangle from his fingertips. "These are all vital purchases, thank you very much."

I give him an incredulous smirk and pull out the crocheted hat. It's striped with a rainbow of colors and has a fluffy white puff on top. I hold it up, spinning it with a finger.

"*This* was a vital purchase?"

"Yes," he declares, using his free hand to pull it onto his head, flattening those golden-brown curls until they fall into his icy eyes. He turns his chin this way and that, showing off his new look. "I needed a new hat for my winter travels."

Despite that odd buzzing energy that seems ever-present between us, I'm . . . comfortable. This back and forth with Oliver is easy, and I realize I hadn't even braced myself for our night together. At this point in the night, I'm usually drained from the effort of having to keep up the conversation, but instead, I'm pleasantly relaxed. At ease even. It's been so long since I've effortlessly fallen into conversation with someone other than Lucy, and even then, sometimes I need my space.

I tip my head to the side, my dark ponytail swishing against my jacket. Suddenly, I realize this could be the opportunity I've been looking for to learn more about his life before Ashwood Haven.

"Do you travel often?"

"All year long. Or, at least, I used to."

Side by side, we continue our stroll through the market, taking a break from the booths and heading straight for the hot chocolate stand. "Used to? Not anymore?"

"Well, I imagine I won't have much time or money for travel now that I have the bakery."

"That's fair. Where all have you been?"

Oliver shrugs again, lips thinning with thought. "A little bit of everywhere."

I snort, grabbing two fresh cups of thick, luxurious hot chocolate topped with a homemade whipped cream that bobs with the movement.

"That was vague. Here, I'll be more specific. Tell me about all the winter destinations you'd take your new hat to."

He blows on his drink, eyeing me over the rim as he seems to seriously contemplate the question. "It depends; winter travel can be a little finicky. If you're looking for a getaway to escape the cold, you can't beat Thailand. Koh Phi Phi is something everyone should experience at least once in their life, plus the markets are every foodie's dream. But if you're someone who likes to embrace the cold, Iceland is the place to be. Between the hot springs, northern lights, and glaciers, you can't go wrong."

My hand pauses halfway to my slack-jawed mouth, the steam from my cup tickling my half-frozen nose. I didn't expect an answer like that. I thought for sure he'd go on about some ski town he visited with a group of friends in college, or maybe a beach trip to Florida with family. Instead, he talks about Thailand and Iceland as if he's been there, and recently at that. As if he's experienced those hot springs for himself.

The thought instantly has my mind spiraling, picturing his large frame poking out from a steaming pool against a backdrop of pristine snow and ice. The mental image has my cheeks heating, something stirring deep in my stomach, and I'm suddenly completely consumed by the need to blow on my drink so I can take the perfect sip. Anything to avoid those steely eyes that must be the same color as an Icelandic sky.

"So, what are you?" His voice lowers as he leans in closer and removes his new hat from his head as if about to share a secret. The air between us thickens, and this time, I know exactly what it is. *Magic.* "A beach or glacier kind of woman?"

Briefly, I meet his gaze before quickly looking away and starting our stroll once again. Putting space between us has the magic settling, making it easy to breathe once again. "I don't know. I've barely left Ashwood Haven, let alone enough to have preferences. I'm not particularly adventurous."

He side-eyes me. "Huh. You don't strike me as the homebody type."

I chuckle sheepishly. "Well, that goes to show how little you know me. My perfect vacation is a staycation where I curl up on my porch every morning with a book and a cup of coffee."

He eyes me warily. "That doesn't sound very exciting."

We stop at a booth, and I make a show of examining the crystals on display. I finger a rose quartz heart, tracing the smooth, cool curves, and shrug. "I disagree. Losing yourself in a good book is the opportunity to live a thousand lives and visit a thousand new places. In the time it took you to climb the nearest mountain, I've ridden dragons, been swept away in a whirlwind romance, and defeated villains on a battlefield. That sounds pretty exciting to me."

I glance up from beneath my lashes to find Oliver studying me with a pleased gleam in his eye and the shadow of a smile on his lips. "Oh, I'm not disagreeing that books give you a chance to escape. But don't you ever want to experience those things in person? Or at least the closest thing?"

His warm, deep voice wraps around me, making my stomach flip in all sorts of chaotic ways. Swallowing the feeling, I cock my hip to the side and give him my best insolent smirk. "I fail to understand how a trip to Thailand will help me understand what it's like to ride a dragon."

Oliver laughs and shakes his head. "Okay, maybe not that. But there are so many other things in life worth experiencing."

"Like?" I wonder, regretting it the moment he leans in closer, making my heart hammer against my breastbone until I'm sure he can hear it. I hold my breath when his gaze flits to my lips, ever so briefly, as if that's where he'll find the answer to my question.

His fingers brush mine, and he grabs the rose quartz heart, holding it up in the small space between us. "Love, for one."

With a deep, shaky breath, I push down the way his words make my heart (and other areas) clench with anticipation. I barely know this man, yet I'm already wondering what he could mean by the word *love*. Is he talking about the feeling, a person, or something more physical?

Clearing my throat, I pluck the crystal from his fingers and hold it up for emphasis. "We have love here in Ashwood Haven."

The corner of his lip curves, showing off that dimple once again. "I don't doubt it."

For several breaths, we remain like that, nearly chest to chest, my heart beating so fast it could be a hummingbird's wings. But I refuse to be the first to look away, to give in and reveal how off-balance he's made me. With our eyes locked, something flutters in my chest, making my heart thud so hard it hurts.

I recognize the sensation immediately.

The town's magic is bubbling again, and the sound of someone shrieking breaks the tension between us.

In unison, we spin around, searching for the source of the outcry. The flutter of magic draws me toward two familiar girls standing at a soap booth, though I can't quite recall where I know them from.

"Rach, what is going on? Are you having a stroke?" one cries, eyes wide and round.

Her friend is holding a hand over her mouth, seemingly frozen.

I shove my drink into Oliver's hand and hurry over, not quite running to avoid adding to the panic. The last thing I need is to cause another scene and draw Stacy's disapproval once again.

I plaster a friendly smile onto my face, doing my best to sound calm. "Hi, is everything okay?"

The first girl shakes her head frantically, never tearing her gaze from her unmoving friend. "I don't know. I don't know what she's saying. It's like she's lost control of her tongue."

My mouth falls open, but no words come out. I have absolutely no idea how to respond to that, and it takes me what feels like forever to compose myself enough to turn to her friend. She's shaking like a leaf but is otherwise motionless, as if moving will somehow make the whole situation worse.

"Hon," I start, channeling Grandma through my voice, "can you tell me what's wrong?"

The girl shakes her head so hard I fear she'll give herself whiplash.

"Okay, okay. Take a deep breath for me," I coo, demonstrating how I want her to breathe until she follows along and calms herself down. I reach up and gently pull her hand from her mouth. "Can you tell me your name?"

The girl takes another shaky breath and then opens her mouth. Out tumbles the most nonsensical string of sounds and syllables I've ever heard in my life. It's how I imagine a Dr. Seuss character would sound, and it takes everything in me not to burst out in a horrified laugh.

The first girl shrieks again. "See!"

I look for Oliver and find him already at my side. The stream of sounds that could vaguely be considered speech didn't resemble any language I've ever heard, but being so well-traveled, he'd know better than I would.

"Do you recognize what language she's speaking?" I ask him before turning to the first girl. "Does she speak any other languages?"

The girl shakes her head, dark curls falling into her eyes. "I mean, we took Spanish in high school together, but that is *not* Spanish."

"Oliver?" I plead, hoping for some kind of answer that makes sense.

Brows furrowing, he looks somewhere between perplexed, horrified, and stunned. It takes him a moment to compose himself, swallowing hard and shifting on his feet.

"Say something else. Have you bought anything tonight?"

She opens her mouth to answer, and once again, a nonsensical cacophony of squeaks and wordless sounds comes out. Instantly, she bursts into tears. Her sobs are more akin to a warble, and that only makes her cry uncontrollably until she's weeping so hard I'm worried she's going to make herself sick.

I look at Oliver, but he just shakes his head. "I've got nothin'."

I wrap an arm around the sobbing girl in my best attempt at comfort. "Maybe we should find a nurse or doctor or—where did you get those?" I point at the coffee cups the first girl desperately clutches, recognition washing me with dread.

"Umm . . . the bookstore? Why? What's wrong with them?" She holds them at bay and studies them as if whatever caused this will jump out of the cup and attack her.

And then it dawns on me why the girls look familiar. They are the same two I saw coming out of my shop while waiting for Oliver.

"No, no, nothing's wrong with them," I lie, "but I think I know who can help us." I lead the girls back toward Moonlit Pages, mentally begging Lucy to remember what charm she'd used on their drinks.

"Is everything alright over here?"

My heart drops through the bottom of my stomach. I stop our small group so that I can turn and face Don, who is hovering nearby with hands on his hips.

"Everything's fine," I lie, my voice cracking ever so slightly. "Just a little overwhelmed. We're all going to hang out at the store for a little while to catch our breath."

Don's eyes narrow before sliding to Oliver and giving the new guy in town a once-over; the drawn-out analysis makes me jumpy, because as lovable as Don is, one thing he takes very seriously is Ashwood Haven and its reputation. He wasn't kidding when he said all Oliver had to do was run an honest business and stay out of trouble, and so far, he's been right smack dab in the middle of trouble since he got to town. I have no reason to believe it's intentional by any means, but Don won't see that. All he'll see is problems for the town and Oliver standing nearby.

"Uh-huh," Don grunts before turning his attention back on me. "Well, I trust you to take care of things, but you know where I am if you need anything."

I soften at his concern, sounding more like an overprotective father figure than the town's mayor.

"I do," I assure him, turning back to my small group of

distressed girls . . . and Oliver. Before Don has a chance to tag along, I usher everyone out of the market and back to the store, willing this all to be an easy fix.

Chapter Six

Lucy and I stand side by side, arms crossed, staring at the open spell book behind the coffee bar counter, the way TV detectives watch a suspect through the one-way glass of an interrogation room.

"You're *sure* you did it right?" I question for what feels like the dozenth time.

Lucy huffs, annoyed. "Of course I did. I know it's been a hot minute since I've cast a communication charm with a friendship focus, but I followed that spell to the letter."

The toe of my boot taps against the wooden floorboards as my lips purse and I side-eye her.

Lucy turns to face my skeptical gaze head-on, crossing her arms as if to say *try me.* I study every inch of her. From the top of her fiery hair to her heavily studded ears, and all the way down to her platform combat boots. With a sassy quirk of her lips, she takes my scrutiny, tapping her polished fingernails against her bicep.

After a tense moment of silence between us, I meet her eyes

again. "Luce, I swear . . ." I warn her, and she throws her hands in the air.

"Look, I know I'm not exactly employee of the month, but I would *never* pull something like that."

I quirk an eyebrow at her, and she softens, conceding a hair. "Fine, I would never pull something like that on a tourist—and especially not this close to Halloween. Magic always acts a little nutty this time of year, and I'm not about to risk that shit becoming permanent."

I sigh through my nose, turning my attention back to the book lying open on the counter.

Despite all the evidence to the contrary, I believe her. Lucy might be a bit of a wild card, but I've always been able to tell when she's lying. The horrified look on her face last night when I brought the gibberish-speaking girl into the shop was completely genuine. But no matter how I rack my brain, I can't think of another explanation.

Unless . . .

As if she can read my mind, Lucy worries at her lip before asking, "You don't think something's wrong with . . . the *book* . . . do you?"

I shake my head, but I'm not sure if I'm answering her question or so utterly lost for an explanation that I can't find the words. The air between us and the book is thick with tension, as if it's luring us in like bait on a hook we know we shouldn't bite.

"I can't figure out how that's even possible. It's a *book*. It can't change its own spells"—I pause, briefly meeting her concerned gaze —"right?"

Lucy's lips press into a thin line and she leans a hip against the counter as black and purple nails click against the granite with thought.

"I mean . . . it did come from Grandma."

"I know it did, but it didn't just come from her." I wave a hand at the yellowed pages for emphasis. "It's been passed down for generations. Grandma wasn't afraid to mess with magic, but I can't imagine her ruining something like our family book for a few laughs beyond the grave." I glance around the shop as if something else could possibly explain last night's charm gone wrong.

"All the ingredients are good, right?"

Lucy gestures at the line of spices and toppings before letting her hand fall against her hip. "It's all fresh."

"And you had full consent?"

"The girls came in and asked for the Witch's Market special, which we agreed would be our Cast-A-Wish Latte. They both ordered caramel macchiatos and asked for their friendship to withstand going to different colleges or whatever. So, I thought an open communication spell with an emphasis on friendship would be what they needed. They'd have some good talks over the course of the festival and then make an effort to stay in touch going forward. That's as close to consent as you can get in this business. Plus, you and I both know that lack of consent would backfire on me, not them. And I'm the one speaking perfect English."

Everything she's telling me matches what the girls told me last night, once we got them all calmed down. After we reversed everything and compensated each of them with a free book and a promise of free lanterns at the Enchanted Lantern Walk tonight, of course. If they don't go tell the entire world about what happened, I'll be amazed; I can only hope no one believes them, and that it fades away before the rumor of actual witchcraft catches fire.

"Maybe it wasn't the drinks. Maybe the festival did something. Was anything weird at the market?" I can feel Lucy grasping at straws, and I wish I had something better to offer her.

I shake my head and proceed to run through the entire night, right down to the strange flutters of magic.

"And . . . that happened while you were talking to Oliver? About what?"

I look away, trying and failing to hide the heat rising to my cheeks at the memory of my conversation with him last night.

We have love here in Ashwood Haven.

I don't doubt it.

My stomach flips all over again, his deep voice so clear in my head that it sends shivers over my skin. I pull the sleeves of my long-sleeve shirt down over my hands, the roll hem stretching between my anxious fingertips.

"We were just talking about travel."

Lucy's entire face screws up into a skeptical recoil. "Travel? You've never traveled more than a few hours from here."

I shrug, using my thumbnail to pick at an invisible spot on the counter. "I could travel."

The red-haired barista looks unconvinced. "To where? Across the county line?"

"You know what?" I counter, meeting her challenge head-on to avoid furthering this conversation as much as possible. "My desire to or not to travel is not the focus here. *I'm* not the one who practically hexed someone last night."

"You sure about that?" she mutters under her breath.

"Excuse me?"

"It just seems like there's a common denominator here, and it's not me."

"I didn't make their drinks last night," I bite at her.

"No, but you were there when the charm went wrong. Just like you were there when the books started throwing themselves off the shelves, and when the ballerinas started flying, *and* when the skeletons started dancing!" She lists off each event on her fingers, her serious exterior crumbling by the time she gets to the last offense.

"This is ridiculous!" I shout, a laugh bubbling out of my chest and up my throat at that absurd list of events. Lucy breaks with me until we've both dissolved into fits of half-exhausted cackles.

"Okay, okay," Lucy starts, catching her breath. "So, we know I'm not messing with the magic, and you're not messing with the magic. That leaves us with one other common denominator."

I groan, and in unison we both say what we're thinking.

"Oliver."

Using a spoon to dump a handful of chocolate chips into her palm, Lucy stares at her hands, a line forming between her brows. "Can guys even fuck with magic?"

"Theoretically, yeah."

"What does that mean?"

I shrug, holding my chin in my hands as I lean against the counter. "Magic itself is rooted in the earth. Some places are more magical than others, and only certain people can tap into them. Ashwood Haven hasn't had a man capable of tapping into the magic for . . . I don't even know how long, but that doesn't mean men elsewhere can't. It's entirely possible that one of them moved here to open a bakery and found himself with a well of magic at his fingertips."

She pops a chocolate chip onto her tongue, humming with thought. "So, what I'm hearing is you need to continue prying into the past of the new guy and find out if he's the one causing all of this."

My heart races at the thought of getting more one-on-one time with Oliver. Normally, being forced to spend time with others makes my chest ache with dread. This time, though, it's rushing with excitement, and it's such a foreign feeling I have to press a hand to my chest to calm the sensation.

The movement isn't lost on Lucy, so I speak before she can comment on it.

"Fine," I chirp, "but that leaves you with research duty."

Lucy freezes, her hand hovering midair on its way to pop another chocolate chip. "Come again?"

"You heard me. We're going to call in Marilyn for backup during the lantern walk, and you get to go look through Grandma's tomes on town history to figure out if anything like this has ever happened before."

"No way. Not happening. Bad idea."

I grin at her, reveling in the way her eyes go round with panic. "Too late. Thanks to you, I'm on new guy duty." I turn away and head to the front door to flip the sign from CLOSED to OPEN, feeling smug as she scampers after me.

"Have you lost it? Do you not remember my two-point zip GPA? I can *not* be on research duty. End of story."

I pause before the front door, whirling on her as Don waves at us, cheeks rosy with cold as he waits for his daily caffeine fix.

"High school was a decade ago. You're an adult, in case you've forgotten. Besides, you and I both know that your crappy grades had nothing to do with your ability to do research and everything to do with your need to piss off every teacher in school by passing tests without completing a single piece of homework."

"But—"

I hold up a hand to cut her off. Don tilts side-to-side, trying to make eye contact and get our attention through the glass.

"But nothing. If it turns out Oliver isn't behind this, then we'll need a lead on what is before Halloween hits and all hell breaks loose."

Lucy glares at me, her mouth snapping shut with a pout. An argument is building in her eyes, and I leave her to stew as I unlock the door and let Don in.

I paste on my customer service smile, but the mischief in my eyes makes Lucy's glare narrow in a dangerous way. "Good morning, Don."

"Good morning, girls!" He steps past me into the shop, rubbing his palms together, and gives Lucy a wary look. He leans into me. "Should I be concerned? She has that *look*."

I suppress a chuckle. Lucy chews on the inside of her cheek, cocking her hip to the side in a way that would make anyone nervous.

I shake my head. "No. She's just upset she has to read a book."

"Ah, well . . ." Don beams at me, giving me his best mayor's smile. "Perhaps you should make my usual this morning, Miss Amelia."

"I'd be happy to." I flash one more smirk Lucy's way before heading for the coffee bar with Don close on my heel to avoid Lucy's wrath.

Chapter Seven

Orange, pink, and purple streaks paint a watercolor sky above the turning trees that encircle the town. A chill from the metal handles of the lanterns hanging from my fingers sends shivers up my arms, and I'm reminded I should have grabbed gloves. Bundled in thick layers, I trek across the brick road to the bakery, avoiding a long stream of people making their way toward the square. Giggling children race down the center of Main Street, their parents huddled together, smiling and chatting as they follow close behind.

Squinting, I peer through the glass door, spotting Oliver as he shrugs on his coat, and with a single knuckle, I tap against the glass to get his attention. The moment he sees me, his face lights up, a gleam appearing in his eye. My heart flutters at the sight, and I raise one of the lanterns, both an offering and an invitation. I can almost hear his breathy laugh through the door as he approaches.

He steps out onto the sidewalk, locking the door behind him. "Another can't-miss event?"

I hold a lantern out to him, letting it hang in the air between us. "With VIP access."

The corner of his lip lifts as his eyes bounce from the lantern to me and back. "Well, how can I say no to that?" He takes the lantern, the brush of his fingers against mine sending a tingle up my arm. "Lead the way."

We weave through the crowd side by side, stepping through the long lines of groups and couples waiting to purchase lanterns and find their place among the growing throng.

"So, how are the preparations for opening day coming along?" I ask.

"Pretty good. Since there were only a few weeks between Miss Laura's closing and the reopening, most suppliers have been willing to work with me and start deliveries ASAP. I already have all my family's recipes ready to sell, so it's just a matter of fine-tuning the details."

I nod along as he talks, pretending I understand anything about opening and running a bakery.

Taking over the bookstore had been logistically very simple. I'd been working at Moonlit Pages for most of my life by the time Grandma decided to step down and let me run it outright. Of course, she'd always been around, giving me direction. Even from the afterlife, it often feels like she's still standing over my shoulder, showing me the way through life. And no matter how I try, no matter how much I tell myself I should do things my own way, I can't help but listen to the memory of her guiding whispers.

The mention of his family triggers something in my mind. I think back to what Lucy said the morning Don told us of Oliver's arrival.

You'd think a guy so interested in maintaining family tradition would take over a family bakery.

The thought of having to force myself into his personal life makes my skin itch. I certainly don't want anyone asking me prying questions, especially strangers. Honestly, I've known most people in this town my entire life, and I still get twitchy when they ask about anything deeper than a spring puddle. But, do I really have a choice?

I use my free hand to scratch at the back of my neck, an attempt to itch away the knot growing from being around so many people. "Don mentioned it's a family business. I'm surprised you didn't take over your family's bakery."

"It's . . . a long story." A heavy pause follows, a dark shadow passing over his face, and immediately, I want to take it all back.

"I'm sorry. I shouldn't have said anything. That was rude of me." I glance at him out of the corner of my eye as we weave around another family and start making our way toward the stage steps. Oliver's blue-gray eyes have gone stormy and distant, as if he's somewhere else entirely and not anywhere particularly happy.

"No, it's fine." He bites his lip, and we walk in silence so long I wonder if he's going to respond at all when he takes a deep breath. "There is . . . *was* . . . a family business. My dad inherited it from my grandpa. Growing up, I always said I wanted to take it over, but when I turned eighteen, I realized I wanted to see the world first. Then, once I started traveling, I couldn't seem to stop. I always said I'd be back to learn the business and take over one day when I no longer felt the need to be anywhere else. But I wasn't even around when . . ." We pull up short of the stage, and Oliver turns to me, though his eyes never meet mine. Instead, they track the lantern swaying in his grip. Stacy waits for me at the base of the stage, checking her watch and tapping her foot impatiently.

Oliver takes another deep breath as if bracing himself, forcing himself to say the words aloud. "It was sudden. Car crash. My dad . . . He didn't make it, and I wasn't there to say goodbye. He left the business to his long-time assistant, who had been working at the bakery for decades."

"Oh . . . I'm so—"

Oliver gives a quick shake of his head, finally meeting my gaze. The storm clouds in his eyes are full of heavy resignation and grief. "Don't be sorry. Alex deserved it. He was a loyal employee, working six days a week at my dad's side. He deserves it far more than my absent ass ever did."

We fall into a heavy silence filled with the weight of unsaid reassurances. My instinct is to tell him that that's not true. That his father was proud of him and probably didn't want to burden him with unwanted responsibilities. That there's more to life than tradition and family legacy. But I can't rightfully say any of those things.

I don't know Oliver or his father; I know nothing of their relationship, and can't speak to what his father thought of his son's travels. And for me, of all people, to speak against family tradition would be hypocrisy at its finest. Isn't that why I'm about to walk up on that stage and lead this year's lantern walk? Because I can't let go of Grandma and what she would have wanted?

So, instead, I wave my lantern at an anxious Stacy. "I should get things started."

Oliver gives me a tight smile, some of the swirling storm clouds in his eyes dispersing. "I'll be here waiting."

Reluctantly, I return his tight smile with a thin one of my own and turn away, feeling as though I received more than I bargained for in that short conversation. I use the few feet between Oliver and Stacy to collect myself, so lost in his words, both said and unsaid, that I don't even remember to be nervous.

"Ready, hostess?" Stacy chirps, herding me toward the stairs and rattling off her reminders. "Tonight is super easy. A simple 'Is everyone ready for the Enchanted Lantern Walk?' And then give the cue for everyone to light their lanterns, and after that, it's literally a walk through the woods."

I barely listen as she talks, throwing one last glance over my shoulder to where Oliver is standing at the front of the stage. He nods encouragingly, and I'm flooded with a strange warmth that makes my heart want to burst.

For weeks, people have been asking me if I'm sure, if I'm ready. All they see is a scared bookworm who'd rather be shelving novels than speaking to a crowd. And if Grandma were here, she would insist on doing this herself.

But for the first time, I feel understood in my need to hold on tight to this responsibility I utterly loathe.

Oliver doesn't hate the bakery, at least it doesn't seem that way. But it wasn't his first choice in life. It's something he's both chosen and been forced into, in a desperate attempt to hold on to family, familiarity, and legacy.

Never in a million years would I have voluntarily signed up to host a week-long event that involved me speaking on stage over and over again. Yet, I can't bring myself to let tradition die. I can't stop living my life the way Grandma would want to be living hers, rather than for myself. Just like Oliver can't let go of his family business, even though he didn't take over his family's business.

I climb the stairs to the stage, approach the microphone, and . .

. hesitate. All the nerves I forgot to feel suddenly overwhelm me in the face of so many. A sea of people watch me, and my heart thrums against my chest, stage fright making my tongue stick to the roof of my mouth.

My fingers reach for the cuff of my shirt, then pause when my roaming eyes find Oliver. There's a kinship hidden behind those eyes that makes me feel less alone on this otherwise empty stage. Because the only reason I'm up here is that I can't let Grandma down. Because I took on this responsibility that she never asked me to. The understanding there isn't just about my nerves—everyone gets stage fright (except Grandma, of course)—but rather a recognition of why I'm doing this at all. Of why I'm putting myself through this, why I took over the Moonlit Pages, and why I can't just let Don host, even if I'm scared.

A weight lifts off my shoulders, and the words come easily, my mouth curling into the first genuine smile I've had while hosting this year's Halloween.

"Is everyone ready for the Enchanted Lantern Walk?" Genuine excitement tinges my words, and the crowd feels it. They erupt into cheers and claps, hoisting their lanterns high into the air.

I lose myself in those wintery eyes, as if Oliver and I are the only ones in the square, as if I'm making this speech just for him. My heart lifts at his crooked grin, and I lift my own lantern into the air.

"Then light your lanterns, and let their glow guide the way."

The magic of Ashwood Haven shudders, a wave hitting me so hard that the only thing keeping me from being dragged beneath its undertow is Oliver grounding me to the stage.

Then every lantern in the square alights at once, flames licking the wicks of every candle. Delighted squeals and gasps echo as the dozens of candles light themselves, as if . . . by magic.

A distant voice, screaming at me from the back of my mind, tells me this is wrong. That nothing good can come of the magic acting on its own like this. But I'm so light and alive that for once, I can't bring myself to care. The magic of Ashwood Haven buzzes through my veins, lifting my spirits so high that with the help of one of those flying brooms, I could skim the clouds with my fingertips. Let the people believe that they are witnessing an amazing display of ingenuity and creative showmanship because, at this moment, I don't have it in me to deny the magic what it wants.

With a burst of energy, I hurry down the stairs, adrenaline pushing me right past Stacy, and instead I rush to Oliver's side.

I skid to a stop before him, so close I brush his chest, rising and falling as he tries to catch his breath. We watch each other, eyes wide, and for a moment, I wonder if he can feel the magic too. His ear-to-ear grin matches my own, and I think he's about to say something when I grab his hand and pull him between people and toward the beginning of the lantern walk.

His touch sends shivers up my spine, and his large fingers weave through mine as if they were meant to rest there. Every second our hands are connected, the magic grows around us, coming to life with a swell so thick I can taste it like a packet of Pop Rocks on my tongue. By the time we reach the start, my heart is racing so fast I think it might leap out of my chest, a sugar rush that has my blood thrumming.

Hand in hand, we pause at the start of the lantern walk, marked by a wooden arch anchored with hay bales and decorated with orange and red flowers. Little pumpkins, both white and orange, are stacked around the base and placed in strategic intervals between little solar lamps marking the way into the forest. Every little detail of the scene before me is more spellbinding than ever before. The little lights glitter, the pumpkins are a more vibrant orange than I remember them ever being, and the glow from my lantern exudes a warmth I've never noticed before.

For the first time in years, the lantern walk feels truly enchanting.

Chapter Eight

It's not until Stacy appears, huffing and puffing, that I finally drop Oliver's hand. The moment our connection is broken, the magic exhales, letting out all the tension it had been building. The world around us dims with each passing heartbeat, until all that's left of the magic's swell is the residual hum of energy between us.

"Amelia!" Stacy cries, gathering herself. "I thought when you agreed to host this year that I'd be in for an easy festival. I assumed there would be no emotional breakdowns like when Andrew hosts or any dramatic pranks and over-the-top grand gestures like when your grandmother hosted, but you are truly testing me."

Even pressing my lips together into a sheepish grin can't stop the giggles that bubble out of me at her dramatic admonishments. "Sorry."

The coordinator's eyes narrow, and she punctuates each word with a tap of her clipboard. "We. Have. A. Schedule."

"I know. I promise, from here on, we stick to it."

She gives me a doubtful grunt but falls right back into coordinator mode all the same. "From here, you just need to lead the walk. The path should be clear, and the actors will be stationed along the way to ensure no one wanders off. Don't worry about—"

"Stacy!" I laugh, giving her shoulder a little shake. "I've lived here my whole life. I've been doing this lantern walk for nearly thirty years. I know how it works."

She glares at me, lip curling as she decides whether or not she can trust me. "Fine. But no more improv."

"I know, I know." I start walking backward into the woods, watching her the whole way.

Stacy taps her clipboard one more time with extra sass, and I roll my eyes before turning my back on her.

Oliver sidles up next to me, strolling along with my leisurely pace and glancing back over his shoulder at the angry event coordinator we're leaving behind. "She really likes that clipboard, doesn't she?"

"Stacy's a wedding planner. A stick up the butt and a penchant for timetables come with the job title. But she's also been the volunteer coordinator for all the town festivals since forever. She's a big part of what makes it all flow so well despite the ever-rotating sponsors and hosts each year."

"Wedding planner, huh? For a woman in the business of happily ever afters, I get the impression that being associated with the person screwing up her timetables is a dangerous game."

"Cause one of these events to start twenty minutes late, and you'll have the most organized murder in history. Complete with an Excel spreadsheet of where she hid the body parts and links to the Google Maps pin drops."

Oliver's lips screw to the side in thought. "She seems more like a Waze woman to me."

I press a hand to my mouth to cover my snort, because I imagine he's right. Lucy has thrown out a few colorful, similar assumptions, but none quite as kind. Like guesses as to the exact type of wood the stick up her butt is made out of and precisely how it got there.

Oliver and I stroll deeper into the woods, a parade of people following behind us at a distance. The glow from the walkway lights is enough for us to stick to the path, but it's the collective luminescence of the lanterns that illuminates the night and gives the forest a mystical warmth.

Through the trees, I catch a glimpse of the first actor.

Lila, dressed in long layered skirts, puffy sleeves, and a corset accentuating her ample curves, leads a bright white mare around a distant clearing. They're far enough away that I can't quite make out the hidden lights among the foliage, but they make the mare and the horn fastened to its forehead glitter like walking starlight. Lila doesn't acknowledge our presence, but I know she's keeping an eye on us all.

The actors tonight have a very simple job: pretend this enchanting setup is their natural everyday life and don't let any of the tourists or children get lost wandering through a dark wood.

Watching her through the trees, I'm transported back to my childhood. When the forest felt so alive with magical creatures, I convinced myself that the only reason my parents wouldn't let me roam the woods at night, no matter how much I begged, was because they didn't want me to get kidnapped by a faerie. Oh, who was I kidding? The faeries wouldn't have needed to kidnap me. They could have simply offered me a sneak peek into their homes, and I would have gone happily, leaving Ashwood Haven behind without a second thought.

Of course, as I got older, I learned that the forest wasn't *actually* enchanted. At least . . . not in the way I had dreamed. All the fae, witches, and unicorns were just neighbors in costume. Still, the whole thing brings my imagination alive and makes me want to go frolicking through the trees.

I study Oliver as we walk, the flicker of lantern light dancing in his eyes and shadowing the hard line of his jaw. Part of me wishes I could trade places with him and experience this whole festival for the first time with fresh eyes. Of course, it wouldn't be the same as seeing it as a kid again, but still, it must be beautiful.

Oliver is the one to break the comfortable silence between us, continuing to match my intentionally slow pace. "Back there, when Stacy was on the brink of a meltdown, she said your grandmother hosted the festival before, but I thought only store owners hosted?"

A small group of teenagers with interlocked arms passes us, giggling and gossiping to themselves.

"Usually, it's the store owner, but it doesn't have to be. In this case, it was, though. Grandma ran Moonlit Pages before I did. It's been passed down through generations in my family. I am simply the latest Moonlit Pages owner."

"How long has your family lived here?"

I shrug. The historical tomes Lucy should be scouring through as we speak hold a record of every generation of my family as far back as we have documentation. Still, I'd never felt the need to commit the information to memory. "I don't know. A stupidly long time, if I'm being honest. We were probably here during the founding of Ashwood Haven, if not before."

The area drew my family because of the magic infused in the earth. It's an innate sense that every witch possesses, like always knowing which way is north; they would have found their way to this exact spot, town or not.

"Wow," Oliver breathes in amazement. "I can't imagine having such a rich piece of family history like that."

"You mentioned your father inherited the bakery from his father, so in a way, you kind of do," I prod gently, trying not to open wounds he so clearly hasn't worked through.

The corner of his mouth curls with thought, some of those storm clouds returning like shadows in the light of the lanterns. "Kind of, yeah—but that's where it stops. My family has been baking for generations. My Papa wasn't the first, but we don't even have a family business quite like your bookstore. Papa started over when he was my age, moved to a new town, and opened his own bakery away from his family home."

Something about that strikes me as odd. Family tradition seems as important to his family as it is to mine, and I have a hard time believing that his grandfather up and started a new bakery for no good reason.

"So . . . you're following in your grandfather's footsteps then. Starting your own bakery instead of inheriting one."

"Yeah, though I'm sure he had a better reason than I do for not taking over his father's business."

"You don't know for sure?"

He shakes his head, locks of golden-brown hair falling into his eyes. "No one does."

"So why Ashwood Haven? Of all the places in the world to start over, why here?"

His lips press into a thin line, brows furrowing as if he hadn't really thought about it before. "It just felt right. After Dad died and I learned I didn't get the business in the will, I felt like I needed to start over and put down roots somewhere new. It was a gut instinct that had me searching for options in this area. It turns out that Miss Laura listed the bakery the day before. I didn't really think through everything. I just knew I needed to get it no matter what."

I watch him closely as we walk, studying every twitch of his jaw and shift of his eyes. I had been quick to dismiss the possibility that Oliver could wield magic, but the way he describes being drawn to Ashwood Haven sounds like a witch finding their way home. As if the thing that brought him here truly is the magic that fizzles like static in my lungs every time he comes near.

But there's no easy way to ask. I can't just blurt out: *Hey, do you have any magical tendencies in your family? A history of casting spells and hexing the neighbors, perhaps?*

No. It's more likely that he has no idea that's why he's here. Like Lucy's family, who had no clue they had a witchy lineage. And yet . . . somehow, he's tapping into the magic—messing with it or amplifying it, depending on how you look at it.

That theory doesn't work either, though. I don't care how much magic he has in his veins; there's no way he could have countered my charms and spells by accident. It's possible that he's been causing it to flare (though I have no idea how), but there's no way he could have thrown out a counter-charm to the flying brooms without knowing it.

As we continue down the trail, I spot Patrick and Rosie bickering in the distance. Behind them is a whitewashed cottage, illuminated by fairy lights and hidden spotlights, vines climbing up the front until they've covered almost the entire wall. The two of them are dressed in classic cottagecore outfits, animatedly arguing and gesturing at a towering pyramid of outrageously large pumpkins.

From here, it's hard to tell that the pumpkins are all styrofoam except for one: the largest, of which they'll start carving here shortly.

Oliver raises a brow as we pass Tilly, who stirs an oversized cauldron overflowing with puffs of dry ice smoke. "Does this town go all out for every holiday? Send a real-life Santa down the chimneys to deliver toys. Pad the entire town for National Bubble Wrap Day?"

A picture of Don trying to wiggle down a chimney in a red velvet costume trimmed in white fur pops into my head unbidden, and I chuckle. I have no doubt he would be the first to volunteer for such a job, even letting that bushy mustache grow into a full-on beard for the authenticity of it all.

Then I imagine Stacy wearing a bubble wrap hat and directing Luke on how to hang banners around the main square. She would lose her mind with each accidental pop, ranting about the deflated bubbles ruining the holiday's aesthetic.

"National Bubble Wrap Day? That can't be a thing."

"Sure is. Look it up."

"Well, either way, the answer is both yes and no. There are definitely some big festivals for the most random of things. We have a flower festival and a winter wonderland festival. The festivals are for the tourists. They get the largest budget, the most marketing, and really bring in a lot of money for the town.

"And then there are the classic small-town holiday events, like a Fourth of July parade and lighting of a Christmas tree, a week-long menorah lighting for Hanukkah, and so on and so forth. But those are just for the locals. Times for us all to come together as a community and celebrate each other. Halloween, however, is the biggest. It's like our masterpiece."

His eyebrows shoot up as he lets out a long whistle. "That's a lot of celebrating. When does anyone have time for the normal day-to-day?"

I screw my face up into a faux expression of disbelief. "Where's the fun in that?"

"I find it hard to imagine people who like each other enough to spend so much time together. Where I grew up, you recognized the people in your class, maybe a few teachers or teammates, and that's about it. Most of the people running our town events were strangers to me, and I grew up there."

I snort. "Well, you'd better get used to it because that's the peculiar place you've moved to. Here, you'll be the odd one out if you *don't* have a personal relationship with the mayor or volunteer to haul a tree on Arbor Day. In fact, remind me to get you the sign-up sheet to deliver pre-dawn meals to those who observe Ramadan. I'm sure they'd love something from the bakery before a day of fasting."

Oliver runs a hand through his hair, blowing out a breath that puffs out his cheeks. "I don't know. Don isn't really my type, but I guess I could arrange a dinner date or something."

My face splits into a wide grin at the mental image of that. I can picture Don and Oliver, two larger-than-life men, sitting at a comically small table, trying to make small talk over salads. Now that's something I would pay good money to witness.

Trying to swallow my chuckles, I nudge him with my elbow. "I'm sure Don will be disappointed to hear that."

But then I start to think about what he said. *Isn't really my type.* That makes me wonder, what *is* Oliver's type? I glance at him out of the corner of my eye, giving him an appraising once-over.

My first thought is someone brave and worldly. The type of woman ready to hop on a plane at a moment's notice, without a care as to where she's going or how much has been planned. The kind of woman who would book the hotel while waiting for her bags at luggage claim because she didn't know what part of Paris she'd be in the mood for until she got there. The kind of woman who would be as content trekking through the Swiss Alps as she would be lounging on a beach in Bali.

But . . . what if it isn't women at all?

Oh, for the love of Halloween. I've been blushing over and flirting with this man, and I don't even know if he's straight. He held my hand before, but what if he only went along with it as a friendly gesture because I grabbed his hand first? I thought he'd been flirting back, but what if that's how he is? Some people are like that. They're so overly friendly and attractive that your mind assumes everything they say is flirty when, in reality, they don't like you any better than their cousin.

The moment I saw him, I automatically compared him to the men in my books. The ones who would burn the world down for the women they loved and worshipped their wives like goddesses. The ones who whispered dirty things like, "beg for it," and growled threats like, "touch her, and you forfeit your own life." I hadn't even stopped to question it.

Heat creeps up my neck and my entire body goes hot with embarrassment as I pull the sleeves of my jacket down over my hands. Before I can stop myself, the question comes tumbling out, completely unbidden. "What is your type?"

The words are more akin to a squeak than a nonchalant inquiry, and his knowing smile makes me want to squirm.

He shrugs, his lantern swinging by his side and occasionally bumping his leg, sending random scatters of orange rays flickering across the dirt path. "Hard to say. I could count the number of relationships I've had on one hand."

My brows furrow. "Really? But you're so . . ." *Attractive,* I almost blurt; the word on the tip of my tongue. Instead, I say, "Well-traveled. I'd think by now you'd have a pretty good idea of the kind of person you're attracted to."

"That's exactly why, actually. I've moved around so much that I've never been stable enough for relationships. By the time I start getting even remotely serious with a woman, I start to get that itch under my skin that it's time to run. To see the next place. Relationships are fun until roots start to form. I'm not against setting down somewhere; I think buying the bakery proves that, but I needed it to be with the right person, in the right place."

I let out a silent sigh of relief when he says *woman,* and I feel a little less foolish knowing I've been flirting with a guy who might actually be attracted to me.

"So tell me, Amelia." Oliver stops, his voice taking on that low whispery quality that feels as though he's saying the words right into my ear. Each syllable is a caress, a warm brush against my skin. His fingers skim the back of my hand, and my breath catches in my throat. His heavily-lidded gaze is both inquisitive and seductive—and completely mesmerizing. "What's *your* type?"

"M-my type?" I stutter, unprepared for this conversation to turn on me. The parade of people following us starts to catch up, and we are passed by groups who side-eye us with an equal mix of irritation and interest. All of them fade away, and for once in my life, I forget that I'm surrounded by people.

"Mm-hmm," he hums. "You've been in Ashwood Haven your whole life and haven't settled down with anyone. What is your type then?"

"I . . ." I start to answer, but the words trail off when I realize I don't have one. I've gone out with most of the eligible guys my age in town and have only really gotten serious with a few, but none of them ever felt like *the one.* So much so that when the last guy broke things off after almost a year together, I moved on in a matter of days. Not because I'm heartless, but because I already knew he wasn't my Prince Charming, so why get all broken up about it?

That didn't stop Grandma from buying me a breakup brownie anyway.

But my options have always been limited to the guys here, in Ashwood Haven—a small town with an already limited population. My type has always been *local,* because that was my only option. It's not like the bigger cities where a single person gets to flip through Tinder, looking for all the right attributes, because there's a never-ending list of other singles waiting to be picked through.

"I don't know," I breathe.

Oliver leans closer until I can make out the individual streaks of iron gray and icy blue in his wintery eyes. Until I can pinpoint each strand of gold in his hair, catching the flickers of candlelight from the lanterns hanging forgotten by our sides.

"Well, maybe we should figure it out together."

He takes another half step closer, and his nearness sends a shiver over my skin. My mouth goes dry, and for a moment, I think he's going to kiss me. The very thought has me holding my breath until my lungs scream in protest. I bite my lip, willing my heart to stop pounding so hard with anticipation because I have only just met this man.

I have no reason to want his lips . . . his full, beautiful lips, on mine. No reason to be wondering if he'd taste like butter and berries and pastries. To wonder whether or not his limited number of relationships limited his experience physically, too. Not that it would matter because I'd be happy to teach him what little I know, and I'd be more than happy to learn whatever he's picked up on his travels.

But . . . oh, hell, do I want him to kiss me. To cross that line with all these people around and take a chance on the little book-worm across the street.

Oliver reaches out, pushing a loose strand of black hair behind my ear, and traces a line down my jaw, sending tingling sensations everywhere he touches.

And then . . .

Every candle, every fairy light and lantern, flickers out, enveloping the forest in complete and utter darkness.

Chapter Nine

The forest is silent for a grand total of half a second before it erupts into chaos. Radios chirp, whispers turn to urgent words, which quickly devolve into shouts. It takes a few seconds for my eyes to adjust to the dark, the waxing moon overhead offering a limited amount of light to see by. It's enough for some blurry shapes and gray-blue shadows, though. Even the solar lights along the edge of the path are out, making the trail ahead almost invisible.

One by one, phones are pulled out, screens lighting up streaks in the night. Flashlights pop up in scattered clumps throughout the trees, and actors prepare to herd everyone back to town.

Oliver's hand finds mine in the dark, warmth melting into me where our skin meets. Deep in my chest, the magic stirs once again. Unlike the previous events, which swelled and crashed like a tidal wave, this is a slow simmer. The tension is building bit by bit, recharging, but for what, I don't know. The prospect of anything else going wrong with the entire festival out in the middle of a dark forest is more than alarming.

I glance up at Oliver and wonder if he, too, notices the flow of energy coursing between our palms. As if to answer my question, he meets my gaze with an uneasy expression.

"Please tell me this is another one of your elaborate pranks that Stacy is going to flip over?" he says out of the corner of his mouth.

I shake my head. "That definitely wasn't me."

"Fantastic," he mutters.

Around us, twigs snap underfoot and boots grind against dry leaves, but no one has taken the lead yet. If no one speaks up soon, people will start panicking. And then I remember with a sigh . . . I'm the host. So, I take a deep breath and amplify my voice as loud as it will go. The magic continues to build until it becomes static in the air around us, making goose bumps pebble across my arms and up the back of my neck.

"Everyone!" I shout, but my voice is drowned out by the growing roar of the crowd.

A whistle pierces the air, so loud my ears start to ring, and I realize it came from Oliver; one of those whistles that only basketball coaches and '70s moms seem to do right.

"Everyone!" I try again, finally getting the crowd's attention. "Please remain where you are. Our volunteers will be coming forward to help guide everyone out of the woods safely."

The throng's rumbling dampens to a hum. They are still uneasy about the whole thing, but their sudden panic has downsized to a containable concern.

Flashlights weave through the trees as the actors surround the long line of lantern walkers. Radio static and beeping underlay talking, and distantly, I hear, "Do we have them all?"

Beep, and then a staticky reply. "Yup. The Jenkins kid was halfway to the cottage, but we've got him back on the path."

"What is going on?!" a familiar voice screeches.

I sigh. *Stacy.*

"Just a little outage . . . of candles . . . I guess," Pat relays into his radio, losing confidence in his report with every word.

"Candles don't have outages, Patrick!" Stacy replies through the static, and the outline of Patrick slumps with the realization that there is no reasonable explanation for what's going on.

I can barely register anything they're saying, though. The magic is swirling so fast that I can hear it like a roar in my ears. Oliver's hand tenses around mine with every passing moment, his grip turning from anxious to strained to almost bone-crushing. But I can't bring myself to pull away, because every muscle in my own body has constricted around my bones until I feel like a spring coiled too tight.

Oliver turns his gaze on me the moment I look up at him, and in unison, our eyes widen, and I *know* he can feel it. I just can't tell if he knows *what* it is he's feeling, but there's no doubt in my mind that his expression is a mirror of my own.

The swelling surge of magic feels as though it's about to burst when a booming voice startles me so bad I jump.

"Miss Amelia."

I drop Oliver's hand to clutch at my chest in an attempt to keep my heart from leaping right through my breastbone. Oliver holds his head between his hands, trying to catch his breath.

Don appears like a specter in the night, dressed in a wizard costume, complete with a pointy star-embroidered hat, bent in half and flopping as he walks. He stops before me, placing his hands on his hips and eyes Oliver carefully.

"Mr. Oliver," he mutters. I didn't even know Don knew how to mutter.

Now that our physical connection has broken, the magic sighs, melting away until it's as if it had never been about to explode in the first place. I'm so relieved I'm tempted to burst into tears, but I can't let myself fall apart when everything is already going so wrong. So, I allow myself a few deep breaths to compose myself before straightening to face Don.

"What's up, Don?"

His gaze flicks to me, but his wary expression doesn't change. "Miss Amelia, you've always been a good kid, so I hate that I have to ask, but you aren't behind this . . . are you?"

I sigh and shake my head. "No," I assure him, "I'm not. I swear."

His lips purse beneath his thick mustache. "Because this isn't something I would put past Stella to set up the moment she learned about Moonlit Pages sponsoring this year. But this isn't funny anymore, people could get lost or hurt, and after the parade . . ."

I squeeze my eyes shut, resisting the urge to jump to Grandma's defense because he's absolutely right. This *is* the exact type of thing she would have found hilarious, and no one in town would have been able to stop her. Not Don, nor even Stacy.

So, instead, I shake my head. "Don, I can assure you I had nothing to do with this."

"I see." His gaze slides to Oliver once again, and I can tell he's putting together the same pieces Lucy and I did this morning.

I open my mouth to defend Oliver, but my phone chimes, and I'm so confused that the words become lost on my tongue. I pull out my phone, double-checking the settings, and sure enough, it's on vibrate. I'm not sure I've ever taken this particular phone *off* vibrate. In fact, I'm not sure I've taken any phone I've owned off vibrate since I graduated high school.

But my messenger app has three notifications nonetheless. All from Lucy.

COME BACK TO MP ASAP!

DO *NOT* BRING THE NEW GUY

But ask about the fritters

THE MOMENT I step through the door of Moonlit Pages, Lucy comes flying out from between bookshelves.

"Finally!" She grabs my wrist and starts hauling me toward the back of the store before I've even had the chance to make sure the door closes behind me. I stumble over my own feet as I wave to Marilyn, who's so wrapped up in her book, she doesn't seem to notice my entrance.

"Hi, Marilyn."

The elderly woman doesn't even glance up at me from behind the register, her chin resting on a fist as she flips through what looks to be a newly released billionaire romance. Her brown eyes merely flick to me over the rim of her thick glasses before returning to her story, her fingers flicking in greeting.

"Come on!" Lucy pleads, tugging at my arm like a kid in a candy store.

I let her drag me away, vigorously shaking my free arm in an attempt to rid myself of my coat as we enter the back room. "What in the world is going on with you?"

Lucy comes to a screeching halt before the basement door, stopping so abruptly that I almost smack face-first into it. Thankfully, I trip and manage to plow shoulder-first into it instead, with all the grace of a horror-movie zombie.

"Ow . . ." I groan, slipping the rest of the way out of my dangling coat.

"You're cursed," Lucy squeaks before going rigid, her frozen stare searching my face for a reaction.

I pause the rubbing of my now-sore shoulder to mull over her words. *Cursed.* The very thought of it feels ludicrous, but Lucy looks so serious, I can't stop the laugh that escapes my throat.

"Yeah, okay. Good one." My laugh dries on my tongue when Lucy's wide-eyed alarm doesn't waver.

"Why are you laughing? It's not funny."

I shrug sheepishly, starting to stutter. "I . . . I don't know, but you can't be serious. Don't you think I'd know if I was cursed?"

Lucy huffs, a shadow of her usual self returning as she props her hands on her hips. "How?"

I throw my hands in the air. "I don't know! That just seems like something a person would notice."

Lucy takes a deep breath, composing herself before the words rush out of her at the speed of a triple-time audiobook. "Look. I know it sounds absurd, but I'm right, so I need you to stand there and listen for a second because you're cursed. C.U.R.S.E.D. Cursed! Well . . . not just you. You and Oliver. Well . . . not necessarily *you and Oliver*, but your families, and—"

"Whoa! Slow down." I hold up a hand to stop her ranting, and her mouth shuts with a clack. "What does Oliver have to do with this?"

Lucy rolls her green eyes. "I just told you. It's not really Oliver, but his family. And your family. Really, it's the two of you together. You're both mentioned."

"What do you mean his family was mentioned? How would you even know that?"

"Same last name." She states it so matter-of-factly that I actually start to question my sanity.

"How do you know his last name? I'm the one who's been getting to know him, and even I don't know his last name."

"Don told me."

"What?" The question comes out more like a cry, my brain starting to reel at how much new information I'm getting in such a short time.

"I texted him." Lucy pulls her phone out of her back pocket and holds the conversation up for me to read.

> What's the new guy's last name?

> Miss Lucy, this isn't the time. I'm busy.

> 😳 😳 😳

> Blackwood

> Thanks!

I cradle my head in my palms to keep it from falling right off my shoulders. This conversation as a whole is making my temples throb, and I want to curl up in bed.

"That is way inappropriate! Where did you even get Don's number?"

She scowls. "Like that's the important thing right now. You're cursed!"

"Okay!" I shout back at her, my voice rising with frustration because she's right. Wasn't I just telling Oliver how he'd be the weird one in town if he didn't have a relationship with Don? If what Lucy is saying is true, then trying to figure out how she got a hold of the mayor's personal number is the least of my problems. I take a deep breath.

"Okay," I repeat at a normal volume, trying my best to compose myself. "Okay, slow down and explain everything."

"I was downstairs going through Grandma's records. You know, as I was *condemned* to do." I give her a flat, unamused stare, but she continues, "Anyway, as I was going through them, I found some old pictures of the town, as well as an article from forever ago about the bakery. It used to belong to a long-standing family when the son who had inherited it a few years prior sold it and moved away, which was when Miss Laura took it over."

"So?"

"Sooo, there was a picture of him from the day he took it over, and I noticed there was a *striking* resemblance to our mystery man across the street. That's when I texted Don to confirm, and sure enough, same last name."

"That is pretty weird . . ." I trail off, recalling everything he's told me over the past couple of days. "He did mention tonight that his grandfather started his own business away from family and that no one knew why."

"See!" She squeals, bouncing in delight at her own competence.

"But that still doesn't explain why you think I'm—*we're*—cursed."

"When I figured out the connection, I started going through Grandma's old diaries from that time to see if there was any correlation between then and what's happening with the magic now." She pauses, worrying at her bottom lip.

"And . . . ?" I prod.

"It was Grandma. She cursed you."

Chapter Ten

STELLA'S DIARY

October 10, 1967

Father's funeral was today. At forty-two years old, pneumonia found his already weakened lungs, and there was nothing I could do. Mama always said those years of factory work when he was young would catch up with him, but the family needed that money to keep Moonlit Pages going, and Father was nothing if not selfless. He took that factory job so his own father wouldn't have to permanently lock those bookstore doors, and where did that get him? Buried beneath six feet of maggot-infested dirt.

I buried him next to Mama and left some flowers by her headstone. She would have liked that, I think. I don't remember her too well anymore.

It's been so long since she passed, giving birth to my stillborn brother. But Father buried them together, so now all three of them can spend some family time together beyond the veil.

All I have left now is Richard.

Oh, how Father loved Richard . . .

October 12, 1967

I've decided I'm not going to let Father's passing be in vain. I don't care what the banks say. It's 1967, dammit! Women can own property, we can vote, and the government says we can own a bank account (like I needed permission from a bunch of pompous men in a courtroom somewhere).

I told Richard, and he couldn't have been happier for me! Said that all my moping around wasn't like me, and he was ready to give me a good kick in the pants if it got my ass into action. And he's right! I know Moonlit Pages and Ashwood Haven inside and out, been working there since I was old enough to shelve books and dust spines. I deserve Moonlit Pages and tomorrow, I'm going to march right down to the bank (well . . . ride down to the bank in Richard's Catalina, but you get the point) and demand they honor Father's will!

October 14, 1967

They said no! Can you believe it? I mean, I expected it, but I just can't believe they actually said no! Right to my face and everything. My goodness, that man couldn't have been more condescending if I had been on my knees!

"Well, if you were married, Ms. Nova," he said as if that matters! Needing a man's signature, as if it were still the 40s. This is 1967! I have every right to own my family's business, and no rat-faced man in a poorly fitted suit is going to tell me otherwise.

To think I wore Mama's pearls for this!

October 15, 1967

I can't believe it. I really can't believe it.

You will never believe what Richard said to me!

I told him of my plan to go back to the bank. That I was going to sit down with Rat-Face, and I wasn't going to leave until he agreed or I talked to his boss and got him fired. No matter what, I was going to get my business before it was taken away.

And you want to know what he said to me?

He said we should get married! That we should just get married and he would sign the papers so that I could keep Moonlit Pages and avoid all this nonsense. As if that was the point!!

Men, I swear!

I told him I would never give in to such an archaic line of thinking and that I deserved to own Moonlit Pages as much as he deserved to own The Daily Bread. He took over the bakery a couple of years ago after his daddy died, and do you think any rat-faced man told him no? NO! He went and signed those papers just like that! No hassle, no condescension.

But I have to be married. I have to have a man sitting next to me and patting my head like a child, making sure I stay in line.

Well, I'm not going to let anyone dictate how I run my own business. Damn them all, I'm going to do this my way.

October 30, 1967

Oh, if it hasn't been the most awful day . . . worse than awful! I swear, I could go crawl right into the grave next to Father and die from heartbreak.

I asked Richard to drive me back to the bank today. I thought for sure today would be the day. I've been there every day for the past two weeks, sitting at Rat-Face's desk and refusing to leave. I told him I'd be back every single day until I got my family's bookstore, and I meant it. Of course, that meant I needed Richard to drive me, but he just had to drop me off in the morning and pick me up after the bank closed. No big deal. William could run the bakery for a little while each day.

But he said no! He said this was getting out of hand and that we planned to get married anyway, so we should just do it and put an end to all of this. I swear, I could have slapped him right there. But I didn't! (Just to make that clear)

I explained to him (yet again!) that this was about more than "getting it over with." I want to own my family's business. I don't want anyone to think I need a man to take care of me and tell me what to do. I am just as capable as him, and the moment we get married and he signs those papers for me, I would be telling the world that I need a man to approve all my decisions.

He said it shouldn't matter what people thought! That as long as I get to keep Moonlit Pages and run it how I want, because he would let me (L.E.T. M.E.) run it how I want, then why did it matter how we got there?

He just doesn't get it!

How could he? He's a man, and everything has been so easy for him! This world was made for him. He's never had to lay a path for himself brick by brick while people stood in the way, making the mortar go hard before you've even laid the next block. If I want people to respect me as a legitimate business owner and a proper part of this community, then I need to prove I have what it takes.

He said that our love should be more important than what people think or what any bank says! The bastard even asked if I even loved him!

I walked right out. Didn't even look back. If that's how he wants to be, then I don't need him either. I'll figure this out all on my own.

Occctoberrr ~~30~~ 31, 1967 DAMMIT!

Sooooo . . . . I found father'ssss ~~wisky~~ whiskey. The goos stuff too! I never did drunk before, but tis stuffsssss good. I like the way s looks.

Sssssssssssss

Sssssoooooo fun to write!

Sssssscrew Richard. His name doesn't have any sssssssss.

I've been thnkin' bout Mama. Bout all the things she taught me before she died—and the book.

Oh, the book! I love the book!

Book, book, book book book boooooook.

Mama said the book sssssshould only be usessed in secret, because MEN don't like ti. It's always the men! Putting us women down.

Well I'll show those Blackwood men . . . we Nova girlsssss don't need em!

From broken heart, a thread is spun,
Two bloodlines bound 'til all is done.
Like moon to tide, their fates align,
A longing deep, a cruel design.

Where flesh meets flesh, the storm will rise,
Old grief shall sever passion's ties.

'Til truths unfold, and masks descend,
Two wounded souls, their stories lend.
Then, the curse shall cease,
And shattered hearts find loving peace.

Chapter Eleven

Beneath the light of a bare bulb hanging from the basement ceiling, I read over Grandma's words again and again. The bulb casts long, dark shadows between boxes of books and all sorts of seasonal decorations and other inventory.

"Oh . . . poor Grandma," I sigh, studying the shaky swoops of Grandma's angry, drunken handwriting.

"Poor Grandma? She cursed two families," Lucy sneers, finally calming down after her big reveal.

"She was heartbroken, Luce." Grandma was one of the proudest people I'd ever met. She was fearless and never let anyone tell her what she could or couldn't do. At least . . . that's what I thought. But these words, this choice to cast a drunken spell, aren't the actions of a confident person. Not really. They reveal her confidence for the front that it was.

On the inside, Grandma was just as broken as the rest of us. Completely and utterly heartbroken, and she couldn't let it show for even a second. As a trailblazing woman of her time, in a time where the world was against her from the start, she had to be strong.

Any show of weakness would have been blown so far out of proportion that she could have lost everything.

Instead, she buried it. She buried the loss of her family beneath a determined front, burying the pain of her breakup beneath a cool exterior. It must have killed her to show up every day without her father, to a store she may lose with a full view of the man she'd walked away from—a man who had been handed everything she wanted.

Who had offered to hand her the same things, only to turn him down so she could hold her head high and know she had *earned* it herself.

My fingers brush the page, hovering over a discolored splotch on the October 30th entry; a tear from the woman who never cried.

"'The curse shall cease,'" I mutter, reading over the curse once again. "She left a fail-safe. She wanted him to come back and fight for her."

"Except, he left instead." Lucy pulls the diary from my hand and flips forward. "Turns out, the spell worked a little too well. 'Old grief shall sever passion's ties.' The magic seemed to take that as a personal challenge, probably because she cast it on Halloween, which, of course, made it all the more potent. She talks about how the bakery became plagued with magical misfortune, making it impossible for him to run his business. She tried to stop it, tried to reverse the spell, but no matter what she did, nothing worked. It needed to be undone the old-fashioned way.

"But Richard left before she could fix things, and since she wasn't talking about her and Richard, but the Blackwood men and the Nova women, it still holds. Which means . . ." She trails off, not wanting to finish the thought.

I take a deep breath, letting everything sink like a boulder deep in my gut. "Which means either Oliver and I need to break the curse, or we're going to be drawn together just to be torn apart."

Lucy nods. "That's the common denominator. Not me, or you, or him. It's the two of you together. As soon as he came back to town, the magic brought you together, so it could tear you apart. And since it was Grandma who cast the spell . . ."

"Oliver will be the one it tries to drive away."

I plop onto a stack of boxes, not caring if I dent the cover of the books within, and let my head fall into my hands.

"And the chances that Oliver has any idea what's going on? Is there anything to indicate he's also a witch? Because that would make explaining this so much easier."

Lucy shakes her head, absently flipping through the pages of the diary. "Not yet, but that doesn't necessarily mean anything. I went straight to the dates from around this time of year, so if there is anything in previous entries that might indicate there's a magical lineage, I haven't gotten to it yet. But I'll keep looking."

My fingers find the hem of my shirt, rubbing the fabric, deep in thought. I need to figure something out before the magic starts trying to drive Oliver out of town and possibly ruin his life. He must have invested so much money into starting this new business. If it fails within the first couple of weeks because Ashwood Haven's magic made his cookies dance and ovens burst into flames, he could lose so much more than a long-lost love. It could send him into bankruptcy.

"So, aside from trying to reverse this thing without breaking it and running right over to spill all my secrets to a guy I've known for less than seventy-two hours, what are my options?"

Lucy shrugs, her lips curling into half a pout. "I don't think you have any. Theoretically, if we can figure out what 'masks descend' and 'their stories lend' allude to, then we can break the curse without telling him about it. Do it all stealth-like. But messing with magic like this, something powerful enough to drive a man to close down his family business and leave his hometown, just days before Halloween, when it's already acting weird? That sounds like a recipe for disaster."

"That just leaves total avoidance," I sigh. "If the magic is trying to force us together just to keep us apart, and I can't reverse it, then I have to fight it until we can figure it out." I must look as dejected by the idea as I sound because Lucy's shoulders slump, and her brows turn down with pity.

"You really like him, don't you?"

I can't stop another sigh from escaping my throat as my heart twists and squeezes until I think it might pop like a sad Valentine's Day balloon.

I gesture at the diary in her hands. "Does it matter? It's not even real."

Lucy's lips purse, twisting to the side in thought as she taps a sparkly black fingernail against the cover of the diary: an expression that never leads to anything good.

"What?" I ask, not sure I actually want to know the answer.

"Well . . ." She pauses thoughtfully. "We could *try* reversing it."

"Okay, that sounds like a tremendously stupid idea. If Grandma couldn't reverse it, what makes you think we can do it four days before Halloween? And with the magic acting up the way it has been?"

"I hear you, but just consider it for a second." Lucy holds out an appeasing hand as she jumps to her feet, suddenly full of frantic energy and a need to help. "All witches know that magic grows stronger every day leading up to Halloween and then falls back to its lowest strength the day after. Grandma cast the curse *on* Halloween, but tried to reverse it *after*. It's possible she didn't have the magical oomph to back up what she was trying to do, and then the bakery boy left before the next Halloween came around. She had no reason to believe he'd ever come back, so she probably let it be. But we are right around the corner from the biggest magical powerhouse of the year, *and* there are two of us." She flashes me a conspiratorial smile.

"Luce . . ." I start, but she gives me those puppy dog eyes I can never say no to.

"Oh, come on! What's the worst that could happen?"

I throw my arms out to the side as if one gesture can encapsulate the entire town. "Um, hello? Have you not been paying attention? Flying ballerinas, dancing skeletons, gibberish-speaking tourists, and a total blackout?"

"I know, but . . ." Lucy bites her lip as if holding back words that she might regret.

"But what?" I ask reluctantly.

"But you like him."

I laugh in disbelief because of all the reasons to risk the entire town's safety, and the festival, that must be the saddest one. "So? It's quite literally magic. If this were a young adult book, it'd be the type of insta love people tear to shreds for being too cliché."

"I just want you to be happy." Her voice becomes quiet and cautious, as if her next words might break what little composure I've been holding on to. "You haven't been happy for a long time."

"I'm happy," I argue, but the rebuttal is weak, my posture falling as I lose all resolve.

"No, you're pretending to be happy. It's not the same thing. Ever since Grandma's health started to decline a few years ago, you changed. You don't smile or laugh anymore. Not really. Not like you used to."

My gaze falls to the floor, and my shoulders start to cave in on themselves. Her words punch me in the chest, and tears instantly start hovering on the edge of my lashes. I want to argue, to tell her that she's wrong. I want to straighten my spine the way Grandma would've done, just as I've been doing every time someone asked if I was fine, but I can't. I've been trying to hide it, to bury the emptiness so far beneath my work ethic and fake smiles that no one would find it. But clearly, I'm not as good at hiding my pain as Grandma was.

Just like with everything else, I can't live up to the legacy Grandma has left me. Not even in this.

"Please," she pleads quietly, a shadow of only moderately forced optimism behind her small smile. "Let's just try."

"Fine." I push myself to my feet, swiping at my eyes as I shake off the weakness I'd let enter my posture. "But if we blow up the whole block, I'm blaming it all on you."

Lucy rolls her emerald eyes and throws the diary down on a nearby box. "Oh, please, like everyone won't be thinking it already anyway."

We both roll our shoulders and shake out our arms as if preparing for an Olympic event.

She holds her hands out to me, and after one last moment of hesitation, I take her fingers in mine.

"Ready?" She beams, a mischievous glimmer in her eye.

"No."

"Oh good! On three. One . . . two . . ." We nod in unison as she counts, never breaking eye contact.

"Three," we say together, and then, as if in a trance, we repeat the curse in reverse.

Reversal spells are always an odd one because sometimes they take all my concentration, and other times, they come as easily as breathing. This time, it feels as though the magic is feeding me the words, placing them on my tongue like precious drops of chocolate. With each one, the air between us starts to hum, a rumble that starts deep in our chests until it becomes a palpable thing in the space between us.

We have to shout the last words at each other as Ashwood Haven's magic—an invisible swarm of swirling energy—surrounds us. The moment we finish, it explodes.

There's no white light or deafening noise like in the books. It's a ghostly force that surges out from where it has gathered in the small space between us. It plummets into our chests and then through us in a wave that has even our hair lifting on a phantom wind.

We share identical expressions of shock and awe as the wave of magic expands out, past the walls of the bookstore and across town with enough force to shake stray dirt and dust from the ceiling. We stand in frozen silence for one second and then another.

"Do you think it worked?" Lucy whispers.

Then Marilyn screams.

Chapter Twelve

We don't hesitate. Within moments, Lucy and I are bolting up the stairs and through the back room. We burst onto the sales floor of Moonlit Pages and pause long enough to pick our jaws up off the floor, trying to process the utter chaos before us.

Throughout the store, books are not only floating off the shelves but also talking between themselves. Except in one corner of the store, where the books aren't so much as talking to a customer, they're arguing in front of her. The dumbfounded woman swings her head back and forth as if watching a tennis match while three thick tomes quarrel over the best high fantasy author.

"If you think George R. R. Martin is one of the greatest fantasy authors of our time, you should go throw yourself beneath the espresso maker right now to spare another unwitting soul from reading your small-minded filth!" a paperback screeches, its pages flapping wildly as it bounces up and down like an irate rabbit.

The aforementioned 'filth' of a book jerks back, its cover

hanging open in the book equivalent of a gasp. "Excuse you! Not all of us were written by a linguist scholar who couldn't even spell, let alone define, the word 'edit.'"

The third book hovers in between, twisting back and forth in time with the stunned customer.

"Are insults really necessary?" the third book chimes in. "I understand you both savor violence, but maybe a more logical Sanderson-esque approach is what our dear friend here is looking for."

"Logical?!" the Martin book shrieks. "Fantasy isn't about logic! It's about whimsy and war!"

"No," the Tolkien advocate pipes in, "it's about exploring cultures and species of other realms as a way of analyzing our own human experience."

The three books all start talking over each other, and the customer simply continues to stand there, completely enraptured by the great book debate of Moonlit Pages.

A yelp from the coffee bar catches my attention, and I turn, only to find that the coffee mug in another customer's hand has started to shake and wiggle. The ceramic mug hums an off-pitch tune that's so atrocious I can't even tell what song it's supposed to be. Assuming it's a real song. After all, I'm not sure what coffee mugs are into nowadays. With an apprehensive expression, the customer slowly tries to set the mug down carefully on the counter, looking as if they're counting the seconds until they can bolt out the door when the mug screams.

The customer jumps, fumbling the mug and nearly dropping it. Coffee sloshes over the edges, pooling on the counter where the customer's elbows lean, the mug in a death grip between their hands.

"I wasn't done!" the incensed mug cries. "How inconsiderate customers are these days. I swear, the audacity of some people to interrupt such a moving melody. And you weren't even going to set me on a coaster or plate? Who raised you?!"

I mentally rank everything going on and decide that Marilyn is the most in need of immediate help. Our elderly part-time employee is standing before the romance section, eyes bulging as she stares at a worm. An honest-to-goodness worm. A worm who is spewing lines from the most graphic, spicy book scenes I've ever heard as if gossiping over Sunday tea.

Lucy beelines for the coffee bar as I head straight for Marilyn, a mutual agreement that while the arguing books are unsettling, they aren't going to harm anyone but each other.

"Well, you know how those tentacled monsters are"—the worm does a suggestive *nudge-nudge* movement—"*so* possessive. Of course, it wouldn't be fun for him unless he used every arm in some capacity. I think that's why, while she was on all fours, he . . ."

"Stop!" I shriek.

The worm pauses, then looks me up and down as if appraising my worthiness.

"And who might you be?" it asks, and I swear that if it had a nose, it would be sticking straight up into the air.

"I'm the owner. Who are *you?*"

The worm recoils as if offended. "I'm the bookworm, obviously."

The bookworm, as if they were hired for the job, and I promptly forgot. I stare at it for a moment, not really sure how a person even responds to that.

"What are you doing?"

"I'm doing what bookworms do, dear. Talking about books.

Just be thankful the book dragon isn't here." The worm rolls its head as if rolling its eyes, as dramatic as a mistress in a harlequin novel. "They're absolute menaces when it comes to a practical discussion about quality. They're far too busy collecting to actually keep up with what's new."

Marilyn grabs hold of my arm, nails digging into my bicep as she looks from me to the worm with alarm. "Amelia," she whisper-yells, "I have been working at this bookstore since long before you were born. I have seen my fair share of odd things in my time here. Hard to avoid with your grandmother around. But this is by far the most inappropriate—"

"Inappropriate?" the bookworm repeats, aghast. "*You* came over here looking for your next read. You seemed lost, so I thought I'd offer some recommendations. As it is, I've read every monster romance in the store—much more interesting than those billion-aire romances you like so much, if you ask me—so who better to guide you in the right direction than an honest-to-goodness bookworm?"

"I wasn't lost, I was debating! I've already read most of these, thank you very much," Marilyn retorts. The insinuation that she isn't as well-read as a worm seems to overshadow the fact that she is, in fact, arguing with a *worm.*

"Okay, okay!" I shout, getting between the two and guiding Marilyn toward the front door. "Marilyn, thank you for coming in and helping tonight, but Lucy and I have it from here."

"Fine, but you tell that worm—"

"I will give that bookworm a piece of your mind. Thanks again. Goodnight!" I practically shove her through the door, the bell above mocking me with its cheery chime.

With Marilyn gone and no one left to argue with the worm, I move on to the bickering fantasy books.

"Oh, for the love of all that is good in the world," I breathe, tempted to follow Marilyn right out that door, crawl into bed, and hope this all takes care of itself before I have to open the store tomorrow. But then, I spot my new bookworm perched on the edge of a shelf in the fantasy section, watching the great Martin-Tolkien-Sanderson debate with rapt attention.

The Tolkien and Martin books are practically page-to-page, and their argument is getting out of hand. The Sanderson tome floats nearby, looking concerned—can a book look concerned?—and seems to sag with relief when I approach.

"I swear these two, I can't get a word in edgewise. And trust me, I have many!" the thousand-page Sanderson tome assures me, following at my shoulder. I decide not to comment on that very obvious assertion and instead head straight for the stupefied woman who still hasn't budged. I place myself between her and the books, getting her full attention the only way I can think to.

It takes a moment, but eventually she blinks a few times, her eyes focusing on me as she comes back to herself.

"Hi!" I chirp, far too loud to be honestly cheerful. With a hand on her shoulder, I guide her toward the front door. "Thank you so much for stopping in, but as you can see, we're having a few issues, so we're going to be closing early. But please do come back tomorrow for a book or two on the house!"

The customer looks back over her shoulder, her blonde braid whipping through the air. "But…how…? The books…They're…"

I laugh nervously. "Ha, yeah. Neat little trick, isn't it?"

"There are no strings," she continues in a faraway voice as if lost in a daydream, "and I touched one. It's not a projection." She turns her glassy gaze back on me and whispers, "It yelled at me."

With a wave of my hand, I do my best to dismiss her concerns, feeling like the very definition of a gaslighter.

"I'm not surprised. Those Martin books can get pretty moody." Because I don't need to ask to know it was the Martin book.

"But—"

"Thanks for coming in!" I cry with a forced smile as I push her out the door. Before I can even close it behind her, the customer from the coffee bar goes flying out the door. They're running so fast that I'm surprised there isn't a dust cloud coming up from their heels.

I hurriedly flip the lock, turn the OPEN sign to CLOSED, and fall back against the door with an exhausted whine. In the time it's taken Lucy and I to get everyone out of the store, several more bookish debates have popped up. Contemporary romance books are fighting with the new romantasy section about what constitutes an appropriate age gap, and closed-door romances argue with dark romances over the definition of consent. Several history books are in concise little groups, debating over the accuracy of obscure details, and the religion section is in an all-out war. The travel section is simply floating around the store from place to place, observing everything like lost tourists.

Not to mention the trinkets, toys, and decorations that have all decided to start their own activities along the floor of the store. Pumpkins are aligning themselves into a bowling lane, the skeletons have started line dancing (again!), and several brooms have started sweeping up little animal-shaped toys like zookeepers herding their inhabitants.

The entire store is in complete and utter chaos, and Lucy is chasing her new professional whipped cream dispenser across the counter.

I close my eyes for a breath to gather myself.

What would Grandma do?

I clear my throat and project my voice over the roar. "That's enough!"

Everything freezes, and slowly, books, toys, decorations, and baristas alike all turn to look at me.

"I want every book back on their shelves by the time I count to five. One!" I hold up a finger.

The books all start talking over each other, and this time, their objections are directed at me.

"Two!" I hold up another finger.

"And what if we don't?" one of the dark romances asks, as defiant and sassy as its heroine.

I narrow my eyes at it. "Any book not back on its shelf in three seconds gets sent back to the publisher."

They all let out a collective gasp.

"Three." Another finger.

The books all slump and slowly float back to their empty slots on the shelves, nestling into their spots among their brethren.

"Four, five." I breathe, letting my hand fall to my side, limp. Every book is back on its respective shelf, and some sense of normalcy has started to return to Moonlit Pages.

"Now for the rest of you," I mutter and push myself off the door, ready to get to work.

Chapter Thirteen

Elbow resting on the counter of the coffee bar, I prop my chin up in my palm and my heavy eyelids flutter closed before I force them back open. Across from me, Lucy puts the finishing touches on a steaming oat milk dirty chai latte and slides it in front of me. I stare at it, using a bit of magic to stir the spoon for me; I don't even have the energy to lift my hand.

After hours of boxing up and relocating lively toys and decorations, a dozen or so one-on-one debates with opinionated books, and the promise of one free worm-sized latte daily, we had the store back in order. Just in time to get an hour or so of sleep before opening the store once again.

With more caffeine than I'd normally consume in a week flowing through my veins, I'd been able to keep up with the morning rush. But now that the afternoon lull has hit, standing on my aching feet seems like a feat comparable to climbing Everest.

As if she can read my thoughts, Lucy's forehead hits the counter with a *thunk*, and she groans into the sleeve of her flannel. I shoot her a sympathetic look as she rolls her head to glare at me out of the corner of her eye, her concealer failing to hide the dark circles bruising her paler than usual skin.

We get only a moment of quiet to ourselves before the bell over the door chimes, announcing another customer, and Lucy lets out something between a sob and a whine. I cringe, smoothing my features into a welcoming smile, and turn to find a large familiar form approaching.

"Oliver," I breathe, snatching my spinning spoon from my cup before he notices its lazy circles.

Lucy's head pops up at a comical speed, and she whips around to watch the new bakery owner approach the coffee bar, pastry box in hand.

He stops to take us in, steely eyes studying our haggard appearance. My mind goes to the newspaper article Grandma had kept from the day his grandpa inherited the bakery. When Lucy had first shown it to me, I'd had a hard time seeing the resemblance. But now that Oliver is right in front of me, wearing an eerily similar outfit of loose gray pants dusted with flour and a white T-shirt, I can admit that she was right. The resemblance is striking.

His grandpa was smaller and leaner, whereas Oliver is all Viking-level brawn. It's like comparing a swimmer to a linebacker. But the smile? The dimples? The eyes . . . those are identical. They even have the same sure-of-themselves smirk.

"Rough night, girls?"

Without a second thought, my mouth pops open, ready to spill everything. The urge is so strong that I have to forcibly shut myself up to keep the words inside. Even then, the desire is almost overwhelming, the words pounding against my lips in a desperate attempt to be set free. Before, I would have assumed it was because of how comfortable he makes me.

Now I know better.

It's the magic. I can feel it pushing us together so that it can drive us apart. Don't get me wrong, the man is attractive, with a smile that makes my heart swoon, but I know now that it's not just my long-dead love life that's making me want him so badly.

I think back to what he'd said about not taking over his family business and how he'd give anything to have the type of connection I have to Moonlit Pages, and I want to be the person to tell him that he does. That he *did* take over a family business, even if he didn't realize it. That I know why his grandpa left Ashwood Haven.

But then I remember why exactly his grandpa left Ashwood Haven, and that I've only known this man for a few days. I have no idea how he'll react to knowing magic is real, that Lucy and I are witches, and that his family is cursed by *my* grandmother. So I keep my mouth shut and hope Lucy does what Lucy does best: meddle.

To Lucy and I, magic is just another Wednesday, but to most people, the existence of magic is simply unfathomable. The last words Lucy and I said to each other this morning before we headed home for an hour of sleep runs through my head.

"Agreed?" she asked.

"Agreed." I sighed. "I have to avoid Oliver until Halloween is over. It's too risky."

"Something like that," Lucy grumbles, straightening her flannel, then her nose twitches. With a deep, long sniff, she comes alive by the second. "Oh my . . . Do I smell . . ."

Oliver smiles down at the box in his hands, which emanates the mouthwatering scent of yeast and sugar and fruit.

"Apple fritters," he finishes for her, confirming her suspicions.

He flips open the top, and out wafts the most amazing scent. Instantly, my stomach growls; it's so loud I clutch at my middle in a half-hearted attempt to muffle it.

Lucy bounces on her toes, clutching her hands to her chest to keep from lunging across the counter and into the arms of the man holding the box of fritters. I think there may even be tears in her eyes. She gets pretty emotional when she's sleep-deprived.

"You're the most beautiful man I've ever seen," she gushes, leaning forward to get a peek inside.

Oliver cocks an eyebrow at me, holding the box out in offering. "Do you want one before she eats the box?"

I bite my lip, shifting on my stool as I stare longingly at the glazed fried dough. I should say no. I'd spent what little time I had to think last night coming up with a plan for the rest of the festival. How I was going to play it cool from now on. No more flirting, no more going out of my way to see him, and inviting him to events. If I did see him, it'd be a quick hello, maybe a smile, and then I'd turn the other way. It wasn't something I wanted to do, but it was for his good as well as the town's.

But now he's here, looking at me with those snow-shadow eyes and speaking with that deep, warm, espresso voice, offering me a box of fritters . . . and I can't do it. I think it might be the most seductive thing I've ever seen in my life.

"Yes, please," I groan, reaching for the nearest pastry.

The moment I grab one, Lucy snatches the box out of Oliver's hands. Before I've even had a chance to bite into mine, she's already moaning around a mouthful of pastry and fruit, flakes of glaze on her chin.

I bite into the fritter and am immediately transported to an apple orchard in the country that's been around for so many generations, even the barn cats know how to make cider. The dough is fried to perfection, crispy on the outside, soft on the inside, with hints of cinnamon and nutmeg, but not too much sugar. All the sweetness comes from the glaze that's melting in my mouth and the chunks of apple that are soft enough not to be raw but crisp enough to add texture. It's fall in a bite, bursting with the flavor of slightly tart apples and autumn spices, and it takes all my self-control not to start making inappropriate noises right along with Lucy.

"How'd they turn out?" Oliver asks, though his tone suggests he already knows the answer.

"They're amazing," I tell him around a mouthful of apples and sugar.

"Better than Miss Laura's?" This time, his question sounds almost sheepish.

Lucy is already eyeing another one as she sucks glaze off her fingers. "Oh, fuck Miss Laura. You can stay."

"Lucy!" I gape at her.

She scowls and waves me off, tearing the corner off another pastry.

Oliver laughs to himself, running a large hand through his hair. "I'll take it." Then he turns his full attention on me, gaze focused on the way I'm licking glaze off my thumb with such concentration it makes my thighs clench. "So, what's tonight's event?"

I swallow hard and clear my throat, sitting up a little straighter. Just like that, a stray crumb on my skirt becomes the most fascinating thing in the store. "Cooking competition. Chilis, pies, barbecue, you name it. Even cake decorating."

He leans against the counter, crossing one ankle over the other and nodding along as I talk. "Well, that sounds like a can't-miss event."

"It is. As a baker, I'm sure you'll love it. Plus, it will give you a great chance to meet the rest of the town's business owners. Like Charissa, she owns the bar and has a beer garden every year."

"Oh, please tell me one of your hosting perks tonight is a free pint." There's a mischievous gleam in his eyes, and it's easy to tell what he's really asking—if that hosting perk comes with a plus one, as it has the last two nights.

I cut a glance at Lucy, who's biting into her third fritter. From behind Oliver's shoulder, she gives him an obvious look and raises a warning eyebrow at me.

I suppress a pout. "Actually, I'll be busy tonight playing judge. You'll have to make the rounds yourself." I try to add a cold edge to the words to make the brush-off clear. Even to my own ears, though, I sound forlorn about my hosting duties.

Out of the corner of my eye, Lucy tips her head and gives me a flat stare.

I can practically hear her voice in my head. *Seriously? That's the best you can do?*

"Oh." Oliver's posture droops all the same, and his dimple disappears, making my heart sink. "No problem. Maybe after?"

It takes all my self-control not to cringe. Instead, I bite my lip, doing everything to look at anything that isn't him because I know I'm one more disappointed *oh* away from taking it all back. There's something about a large man with the eyes of a sad puppy that makes my heart want to snatch him up and make everything okay.

But even in the minutes he's been here, the magic is starting to build. We aren't even touching, and there's a buzzing in the air as if the magic is the villain in an old-timey cartoon, rubbing its hands together with a malicious grin and waiting for its plan to unfold.

"No can do. As one of the judges, I have to stay late." It takes a significant amount of effort to keep a melancholy edge from my tone. Even if I wasn't blowing Oliver off, I'd still be dreading tonight.

Initially, playing the judge at an all-night cooking competition sounded like the biggest perk of playing host. Now, after a night of no sleep, with an already drained social battery, it was taking every-thing in me not to call in sick like a kid trying to get out of a test.

Oliver's brows furrow, and I know I'm being the queen of mixed signals right now. In a matter of days, we've gone from strangers to flirty dates to almost kissing, and now I'm giving him the cold shoulder. He's about to say something else when the door-bell chimes, announcing a customer.

I hop up and beeline for the front desk, desperate for a large group that needs my undivided attention.

Instead, I find a young couple. A young woman in a Halloween-themed dress drops her girlfriend's hand and goes straight for the history section, clearly on a mission. The other hangs back, looking only mildly out of place as she browses the front table filled with stickers, pins, candles, trinkets, and an assort-ment of themed staff picks.

"Hello! Welcome to Moonlit Pages. Can I help you find anything?" I give the woman my cheeriest customer service voice, silently imploring Oliver to take the hint and leave before anything bizarre happens.

She grins back. "No thanks. Just looking around."

My smile turns strained, and I seriously contemplate begging her to let me help her find something, or if that would be too pathetic. Before I can decide, she turns away to go look for her girl-friend. Reluctantly, I spin on my heel to head back to the front desk and find Oliver leaning there, watching me with a dubious expression.

I skirt around him, brushing a stray strand of black hair behind my ear to avoid his gaze and make my way behind the desk. I busy myself with refilling our take-a-chance gum ball machine that gives people a book recommendation at random. At least, that's how it's advertised. In reality, it's been charmed to give recommendations based on the customer's mood. Like a bookish mood ring.

Oliver leans across the desk until we're at eye level and lowers his voice for only me to hear.

"Is everything okay?"

I have to physically bite my tongue to keep from spilling every-thing and instead say, "Of course. I'm just really busy."

Oliver makes a show of glancing around at the mostly empty store before turning his attention back to me. "I'm sorry if I crossed a line last night. I . . . Well, I thought . . . Actually, it doesn't matter what I thought. What matters is that I clearly made you uncomfortable and—"

"Oliver." His name is sweet on my tongue as I touch his hand where it's leaning against the desk without thinking. He stops his rambling, looking so distraught at the prospect of having violated some kind of unsaid boundary that I can't help but comfort him. "You didn't do anything wrong."

He sighs with relief, his entire body relaxing. His hand turns over to grasp the tips of my fingers. The soft pad of his thumb brushes against my knuckles with a gentleness that shouldn't be possible for someone with such calloused hands.

"I'm sorry," he says again. "After you ran off last night, I felt like the biggest ass in the world. I made the fritters as an excuse to come over and make sure we were okay." He snorts, laughing at himself and shaking his head.

Longing pulls at my heart, and my entire chest starts to ache. I can't believe *this* is the man Grandma had to curse. Why did she have to bar me from the guy who's so upset over the prospect of *almost* kissing someone who wasn't that interested? Or so he thinks. Of all the assholes and pushy jerks in the world, it's the one who looks like he stepped out of a fantasy novel and brings apology apple fritters that I'm not allowed to be interested in.

Even as we stand there, mere fingers touching, the magic of Ashwood Haven tenses, ready to lash out at any second.

I pull my fingers from his. "I can't talk right now. I'm sorry, but you need to go."

His brows furrow again, but this time, he looks at me as if he's realizing something for the first time. We stand there without talking for so long that I'm about to ask him to leave again when he whispers, "You can feel it too, can't you?"

My eyes widen, and a whirlwind of emotions stops my heart. Hope that he is saying what I think he's saying. Panic that he might already know my secret. Desperation that he understands what it is he's feeling, and dread at the prospect that he doesn't realize its magic at all. That he can feel it but has no idea what it is.

"What?" I breathe.

A crash and cry of surprise startles us both, and we jump as if a gun has gone off. It takes me a heartbeat to pull myself together before racing around the end of the desk and toward the only customers in the store. I prepare myself for any number of things. Flying books, bowling pumpkins, or the return of Ashwood Haven's newest resident: the bookworm.

Instead, I find the two women huddled together over a pile of books on the floor, giggling.

The one in the Halloween dress blushes, pulling the books into her arms. "Sorry. I'm a butterfingers."

I sigh with relief, a small laugh escaping me as I hold a hand to my chest in an attempt to stop my heart from beating right through my ribs. The bell over the front door chimes, and when I turn, Oliver is crossing the street to his bakery.

Chapter Fourteen

Steam swirls in the chilly night air, carrying the mouthwatering scent of tomatoes, garlic, and ground beef from my ninth spoonful of chili. I'm immediately hit with the sweet and acidic taste of fresh garden tomatoes swimming in a thick, meaty broth, followed by a subtle but noticeable kick of cayenne. The warmth slides all the way down to my stomach, and a toasty heat starts to spread throughout my body, fighting off the frigid night.

I take my time, focusing on the aftertaste lingering on my tongue, before furiously filling my scorecard with quickly scrawled scribbles. Ellie watches us from the other side of the table, trying to deduce the final tally by staring into each of the judge's souls.

I happily hand my card to Stacy before giving Ellie a sympathetic yet encouraging smile. I know she's nervous, but out of all the chilis I've tried tonight, hers is easily my number one, which isn't surprising coming from one of our few full-time firefighters. She flashes me an eager grin, bouncing on her toes and stuffing her hands deep into the pockets of her Carhart coveralls.

Impatiently, I wait for my fellow judges to finish filling out their cards. While this has by far been my favorite hosting duty so far, I'm itching to get to the desserts. So far, we've judged barbecue, mac 'n' cheese, tacos, curries, sausages, and now, chilis. But all the savory foods are over, and it's time to move on to all kinds of pies, cakes, cookies, and my all-time favorite: the wild cards.

The 'wild cards' is a sweets category set aside for desserts that don't fit into one of the five other categories. I always learn about new dishes from all over the world during the wild card category, which usually turns into my year-long fixation. Last year, it was knafeh khishneh, a baked Palestinian dessert consisting of shredded phyllo, sweet cheese, syrup, and pistachios. It was so good that I paid Amir to make it at least once a month for the last year, knowing I'd *never* be able to replicate it, no matter how many recipes I tried.

"Are we ready, folks?" Don asks, clapping his hands together, ready to continue leading our little procession; my fellow judges and I all nod.

"Wonderful! Because this year we're going to be starting with cake decorating, then we'll move on to our wild cards."

Mike flashes me a pearly white smile, the one Lucy and I referred to as the 'movie star' smile growing up. When we were younger, we had the biggest crush on him despite our decade-wide age gap, only to be disappointed when we learned that the reason he married Jim was that we would never be his type.

"I'm so ready for cake decorating," he gushes, rubbing his gloved hands together. "I caught a glimpse of one earlier, and I'm pretty sure it's as big as Sophie."

"That's going to be a sight to see. Do you remember last year with the full-sized tombstone? With grave dirt, moss, and the aging of the engraving? That was impressive."

"I heard," one of our fellow judges interjects, turning to gossip over her shoulder, "that there's been a last-minute entry in the wild cards category this year."

"What?" I gasp, eyes going wide as our small group shuffles forward. "But slots have been closed for weeks."

Simra shrugs, dark brown eyes sparkling with excitement. "I guess they made an exception since he's so new to town and didn't have a chance to enter before."

My shoes turn to lead, halting me in my tracks.

"Ugh, please tell me it's the new bakery owner," Mike groans, his head tipping back as if he's pleading to the gods above. "I need to know if he's anywhere as good as Laura. I miss my Sunday morning carrot cake muffin."

Our fellow judge winks and gives a suggestive shrug. "I guess we'll just have to see."

I don't hear another word they say. I force one foot in front of the other as our small group approaches the massive cakes awaiting our judgment. Just this afternoon, Oliver hadn't even known about the cooking competition, and already he's talked his way into a spot in the most popular category. I eye Don warily, wondering if it was he who gave Oliver the spot and what Oliver had offered as a bribe. I can't imagine Stacy loosening the reins enough to add a last-minute slot.

The thought of being forced into a face-to-face situation with Oliver makes my heart race with anticipation. It's like the scene from a romance novel, where the sexy enemies are forced together by fate and the gods themselves to defeat the evil of the story.

Except in their story, they become lovers, and in mine . . . Well, my gut is already starting to curdle with dread.

Part of me can't help but wonder if this isn't the magic at work yet again. I don't know how influential the magic truly is or how much of this is his choice. I know now Oliver can feel the magic at play between us, but I don't know if he realizes that it's the force drawing us together.

It's at that point in my mental spiral when I internally shake myself and roll my eyes at my own ego.

I've only known the guy for a few days. Why am I so quick to assume that his joining this event has anything to do with me, magical interference or not? Maybe Oliver took my casual mention of the cooking competition and realized what a good opportunity it would be for him to insert himself into the heart of town affairs. What better way for a baker to leave his mark than to win a bake-off mere days before his grand opening?

My gut knots at the thought . . . It would be just my luck that Oliver is only trying to be a good businessman and neighbor, and that the magic would decide this small interaction is enough to go berserk once again—and with all these people around.

Even as I get up close and personal with some of the most amazing cakes I've ever seen, I can't stop my internal battle with my anxiety. I can barely concentrate on the massive Frankenstein head made of layers upon layers of pound cake and caramel apple filling because I'm too busy dissecting every sound at the fair. Every time a child shrieks or someone whoops, I nearly jump out of my skin, waiting for the next magical catastrophe.

Cake decorating goes by in a blink, and before I know it, I'm giving a perfect decoration score to a three-foot-tall haunted house with spun sugar cobwebs, stained "glass" windows, turrets, and a massive vicious-looking jack-o-lantern on top. It's a work of art down to the very last detail.

I'm about to put a forkful of cake into my mouth to see if the masterpiece tastes as good as it looks when I spot Oliver out of the corner of my eye.

Stationed at the first wild card booth, he stands behind one of several glass trays, awaiting our team of judges. His eyes meet mine, and the cake on my tongue turns to ash as my stomach flips. Something in the back of my mind tells me that the flavors are amazing and that the black cocoa cake melts on my tongue, but I hardly notice as all my attention goes to the man standing only feet away.

"How did I not know you could make a cookie-less cake taste like Oreos?" Mike moans, making me jump back to reality. He closes his eyes, slowly licking his plastic fork like the frosting is giving him life. "I'm texting Jim the moment this is over and telling him black cocoa needs to be on our next grocery list."

I give him a nervous laugh, poking at the slice of cake on my plate. "Good luck with that. I don't know about you, but I've never seen black cocoa at the Corner Market."

Mike sighs longingly. "Guess I'll have to stick with Oreos. What a shame." He gives me a quick wink before popping another bite of whipped frosting into his mouth.

I respond with a tight-lipped smile, unable to resist glancing at Oliver out of the corner of my eye.

"Cute," Mike whispers, nudging me with his elbow, "and a baker. Good choice."

I gasp, gathering myself and turning my back on the wild card booth as if there isn't a man over there consuming my every thought. "I don't know what you're talking about. I was just scoping out the best dishes."

He gives me an incredulous look that tells me I'm not fooling anyone. "Sure, let's go with that. Wait! That's the *new* bakery owner, isn't it?"

I push a heavy sigh through my nose, forcing a pleasantly blank expression onto my face.

"Yes," I say with forced patience. "Yes, it is. His name's Oliver."

Mike gives me a knowing, slow nod. "Good for you, girl. You could use a little sweet in your life."

My mouth falls open, and I'm about to inform him that I am perfectly happy single when another unsolicited opinion pops in over my shoulder.

"I'm inclined to agree," Don grumbles, low enough for only our small group to hear.

"Don!" I gasp, unable to contain my embarrassment as heat starts to creep up my neck.

"I'm sorry, Miss Amelia, but I knew your grandmother for many years, and she would want you to have a little fun. Though . . ." Don eyes Oliver suspiciously, giving the large baker a once-over that tells me he's still making up his mind on whether or not he'll be a good addition to the town. "I can't say I approve of your taste."

Despite the cold of the autumn evening, my cheeks start to burn, and I can only imagine how red my face is growing by the second.

"I don't need a boyfriend to have fun," I whisper-yell at them, pushing hair out of my face as I peek over my shoulder to make sure Oliver isn't overhearing this humiliating conversation.

"By the way, I'm on their side," Simra offers, leaning in to join the conversation she was definitely not invited to. She gives me a guilty shrug. "Sorry."

"Oh my . . ." I bury my face in my hands, unable to look at any of them. I know what they're saying is coming from a place of love, but when did my love life become a topic for public opinion? "This isn't any of your guys' business!"

Mike holds an offended hand to his chest, a mock look of hurt on his face. "Are you saying we aren't family?"

I roll my eyes. "Of course not, but—"

From the front of our group, Stacy knocks her knuckles against that blasted clipboard, which I'm beginning to hate, to get our attention. "Okay, everyone! It's time to move on to our wild cards."

As a group, we start to shuffle forward. I glare at each of the three busybodies in turn. "Not. A. Word. Any of you."

Mike locks his lips and throws away the key. Don looks around him as if he has no idea what I'm talking about at all. And Simra smiles in a way that is probably intended to look innocent but comes off as anything but.

Inwardly, I groan, but there's nothing more I can do. I just have to get through this tasting without the magic going wild, turning the Frankenstein cake into a monster, or an overbearing neighbor embarrassing me. All I need is a solid minute or two of pure, normal, uneventful bliss.

That's all.

I sigh. I might as well be asking for snow in July . . .

Don approaches Oliver's table, hand outstretched. "Good to see you staying out of trouble, Mr. Blackwood. I'm glad you were able to join us as we discussed. I was worried you'd be too . . ." Don's eyes narrow, the last word a clear accusation. "Busy."

Oliver grabs Don's hand, giving it a good, hard shake the way guys do. "Of course. Holidays like this are so important for bringing the community together. What kind of local would I be if I didn't get involved?"

Though he tries to hide it, I catch the almost imperceptible sarcasm glaze over his words and can't stop the smirk that curls my lip. He's using our conversation from yesterday to his advantage, and I can see right through it. Something I make clear when his eyes flick to mine, and I give a minute shake of my head. The guilty little lick of his lips and small breath of a laugh tell me I'm not wrong.

And yet . . . I can't look away. There's something so endearing about the way he's charmed my fellow townspeople. In a few days, he's already developed a fan club of people watching his every move. I can already picture him signing up for decorating committees at Christmas and setting up his own booth at the Witch's Market next year.

"I'm so glad you were able to join us for our cook-off," Stacy starts, her smile strained as she studies her clipboard and adds under her breath, "even if it was last-minute."

Oliver's neck strains with guilt, looking like a scorned child, and I have to hide a smile behind my hand.

"That's on me, Miss Stacy," Don interjects, jumping to Oliver's defense. "I made an exception for our newest neighbor to help him start his business off on the right foot. Don't take it out on the poor boy."

Stacy takes a deep breath before plastering on the fakest patient smile I've ever seen. "Of course. Anyway"—she turns her attention back to Oliver, making a point of giving Don the cold shoulder—"please tell our esteemed group of judges what you've made for us today."

Oliver tries and fails to hide a laugh at the two's bickering as he rubs his hands together and looks down at the dishes laid out before him.

"Today I have fall-themed oyster baklava bites. Please, don't be fooled by the name, the oyster part refers to its shape and shape alone." I can't help but giggle at the sighs of relief from at least two or three of my fellow judges. "Now, as you all probably know, a traditional baklava is primarily made of phyllo dough layered with sweetly spiced nuts and drenched in a honey syrup. This particular baklava is still made with phyllo dough, but instead of pistachios, I've used a combination of pecans and walnuts, spiced with a mix of ginger, cloves, and cinnamon. And instead of a traditional honey syrup, I've used a homemade pumpkin spice maple syrup honey mix. Fall in a bite. Please enjoy."

As a group, we all step up to the table, eagerly taking a perfectly bite-sized piece of baklava. Oliver's gaze never leaves me as I approach the table, and there's something intimate about the way he watches me bite into my piece. The moment the baklava hits my tongue, my taste buds come alive, and I have to close my eyes to take in all the distinct layers.

The first layers of phyllo are crispy, giving way to dense layers of still slightly crunchy nuts and a thick bottom layer that's been soaked in the pumpkin spice syrup. It's so sweet that this one bite feels almost sinful, but there are undertones of brown butter that add depth to the nutty layers. Then there's something . . . else. Something tingling across my tongue that I almost miss. It takes me a second to identify what it is that has me sucking sticky remnants of syrup off my fingers, and the moment I figure it out, my eyes fly open.

I whirl on Oliver, only to find him already watching me closely. Our gazes lock, the corner of his lip lifting in a knowing smirk. I feel as though I've been caught in a lie, laying my deepest darkest secrets bare for him to see.

Magic. He used magic to enhance his flavors, giving them an almost addictive quality. And the look on his face says that he can see that very realization written across my face, as easy to read as a large-print book.

For days, I've been wondering how much Oliver knows about magic and the witchy heritage of Ashwood Haven. Now, there's no denying it. Oliver is a witch, able to tap into Ashwood Haven's deep well of magic.

All around me, my fellow judges start to swoon, uttering accolades and moaning about placing future orders as soon as possible. I know without question that Oliver will be this year's esteemed wild card champion.

Which also means he'll be receiving the same prize as all the other category winners: A cash prize and a ticket to tomorrow night's movie fest as *my* VIP guest.

The realization sinks like a rock in my stomach, and I wonder if he understands what exactly it is that's happening . . . how many people he's put in danger.

I really suck at this whole total avoidance thing.

Chapter Fifteen

The next morning, I make my usual trek from my house to Moonlit Pages. Instead of opening the door for Lucy, though, I march straight across the street to the bakery. She's close on my heel as I stomp along the brick road, dry leaves crunching underfoot, and approach the glass door with my hands fisted deep in my jacket pockets.

"Hey, hi! Where are you going?" Lucy rushes after me, trying to get my attention as she pulls her jacket's sleeves down over her hands and burrows her chin into the checkered fuzz. "I don't know if you've noticed, but it's basically freezing, and you have the keys to the nice warm store. This might not be the best moment to bring it up again, but if you gave me back my keys, this wouldn't exactly be a problem. I know you didn't approve of me and Grandma trying to summon a poltergeist, but—"

I cut her a glare that puts an abrupt end to her early morning rambling and pound the side of my fist against the wooden frame of the bakery door as if it's offended me. Lucy stares with wide eyes, glancing between me and the door as it rattles on its hinges.

"Did something happen last night?" she asks carefully, drawing out the words.

Normally, she would have been the first person I called after learning that the new guy in town is not only a witch but is also using magic to cheat his way into the town's heart. After the last few days, I gave her the go-ahead to close the shop at normal hours so she could go home and get some sleep. Meaning not only did she have no idea what was going on, but I had been left alone with my thoughts to mull over this new revelation.

At first, I felt relieved. Oliver's knowledge of magic made it so much easier to explain what was happening . . . but the longer I lay awake in my bed, staring at the ceiling and replaying every moment since he arrived in town, the angrier I became. This whole time, I've been at my wits' end trying to navigate Ashwood Haven's increasingly temperamental magic, and he's over here sprinkling it onto desserts like powdered sugar to win a stupid cooking competition.

I huff through my nose and whirl on her. "He knows."

Lucy takes a step back, shooting me a wary look. "Knows . . . what exactly?"

"The magic. He knows about the magic. He's a witch."

Lucy's jaw drops, and she spins around, double-checking our surroundings to make sure I'm not angrily outing us to a bunch of tourists, but as per usual, the street is empty this early in the morning.

"Oliver!" I shout, irrationally angry that my pounding on the door hasn't gotten his attention yet.

"Have you lost your mind? Keep it down!" Lucy whisper-yells at me, continuing her vigilance of the street, as if Stacy is going to jump out of the nearest alley to scold us for throwing off her circadian rhythm.

Finally, the man of the hour makes an appearance. He doesn't look alarmed or surprised by my pounding on his door, though. If anything, he looks resigned to his fate—like he's been waiting for this confrontation all night.

The moment he opens the door, I storm inside, pushing right past him until I'm pacing across the black and white tiled floor.

He and Lucy exchange a loaded look as he waves her through the door.

"Please, come on in. I was just doing some prep. Would you like a scone?" Sarcasm drips from his words like honey as he closes the door behind her.

"You cheated," I announce.

Oliver scoffs, pushing his hands deep into his gray work pants. "You're joking, right?"

I cross my arms, popping my hip to the side to emphasize my irritation. "Of course I'm serious. You used magic to win the cooking competition. That's an unethical use of magic and gives us all a bad name."

Oliver gives Lucy a *she can't be serious* look, while Lucy's face falls into a deadpan stare that tells me I'm focusing on all the wrong things here. The truth is, I know I'm focusing on the most absurd part of this whole situation. I just don't care.

After a long moment of silence, I flinch beneath their scrutiny, dropping my gaze to the toe of my boot.

"Fine," I concede, "but you did cheat."

Oliver rolls his eyes. "You're a witch, and this whole town is drenched in magic that's losing its mind. How about we discuss that instead?"

Lucy's expression strains as she steps forward. "Okay, I don't think I need to be here for this, so before you two get too deep into this much-needed conversation, I'm just going to take the keys . . ." She lets the words trail off, holding out her hand expectantly.

"Oh no," Oliver scolds, and Lucy grimaces. "I get the feeling you're as wrapped up in this whole thing as we are."

Lucy's lips press into a thin line, and she turns on the heel of her combat boots. "Kinda, sorta, not really."

He raises an eyebrow at her. "Are you a witch too?"

"Yeah, but see, I'm not cursed so . . ." She turns back to me. "About those keys."

My eyes bulge at her slip-up.

What? She mouths at my gawking, utterly unaware of what she just said.

"Excuse me"—Oliver leans forward as if maybe he didn't hear her right—"cursed?"

I sigh as Lucy cringes.

"Nice one, Luce," I breathe.

She whispers an apology as I drop the store keys into her outstretched hands and shuffles out the door, sparing Oliver an apologetic glance. He closes the door behind her, leaning against the glass with one hand and pinching the bridge of his nose with the other.

The silence that follows is heavy with unsaid thoughts as Oliver runs a large hand over his face, looking around the bakery as if the answers he's seeking will write themselves on the walls.

"Cursed," he repeats, as if dissecting every acidic flavor note of the word. I guiltily shift back and forth on my feet and watch as he starts to pace, deep in thought. "By any chance, does 'cursed' mean something different to you guys than I was taught growing up?"

Knowing who his grandpa was . . .

"Probably not," I admit.

He sighs, a heavy chest-caving sigh that speaks of a bone-deep exhaustion, then he pulls out a chair and props himself on it and gestures toward me. "Please, start from the beginning."

I take a deep breath. "Do you remember how you told me you wished you had a bakery like Moonlit Pages, passed down through generations and steeped in family history?"

He nods, chin resting in his palm.

I hold my hands out to encompass the whole of the bakery storefront. "Well, congratulations. You do."

I let my arms fall to my sides with a *thump*, but Oliver only blinks at me, unamused.

"What?"

"During the lantern walk, Lucy was down in the basement of the shop and found one of my grandma's old diaries. Turns out she had quite a thing with the bakery owner across the street when she was younger. Richard Blackwood."

Oliver straightens at his grandfather's name, his gaze darting around the bakery before landing on me once again. "Wait . . . You mean . . . ?"

I nod. "This bakery *was* your grandfather's." I take a deep breath before saying the next part. "I know why he gave up the family business. I know why he left Ashwood Haven."

Oliver's eyes go wide as he stands, mouth falling open. "Why? What happened? Why didn't you say anything?"

"I've been trying to figure out how to tell you, but I didn't know how much you knew about magic and Ashwood Haven, which made the whole process of telling you about the curse really hard. I'll show you everything we've found; it's not much, but if you want to read it all, you can. But the short of it is that Grandma and your grandpa dated for a while when they were younger. They were pretty serious, talking about marriage and starting a life together, but then her dad died, and she had to fight to keep Moonlit Pages. In the end, they wound up breaking up, and in a drunken rage, Grandma cursed your grandfather. At least, that's what she was trying to do."

"What did she actually do?"

I hesitate, biting my lip. "She ended up cursing our families. Basically, the magic of Ashwood Haven is trying to force us together so that it can tear us apart. That's what drove your grandfather out of town: the magic. It caused a ton of problems for him and made it impossible for him to maintain the business, so he left. And if we can't keep some distance between us, it will do the same to us. Or, more specifically, you."

He sighs. "Because your grandma cast the curse."

I nod in answer, even though it isn't a question.

Oliver's winter gray eyes take in the bakery around him once again, as if seeing it through the decades, all the way back to when his own grandfather stood behind the counter. Together, our eyes land on the display case, and I can see it so clearly, it's like he's right there. A younger, leaner version of Oliver, carefully placing biscuits and bagels and bread loaves in rows behind the glass. I can see him smile, Oliver's same dimple in his cheek, and it makes my heart ache for what could have been. For what Grandma lost.

Oliver leans over, laying a hand on the wall, as if he can sense his own family history steeped in the very wood and brick.

"Can we break it?"

I grimace, thinking about the bookworm who will be scooting along the coffee bar as we speak to get its daily latte. "We . . . tried. It didn't go as planned."

Oliver quirks an eyebrow at me in question.

"It backfired."

His lips press into a thin line, and he gestures toward the back of the bakery.

"That explains my new talking sourdough starter."

I gawk at him. "You have a *talking* sourdough starter?"

"I do now," he grumbles, glaring at the back room.

"Not that he's cared to introduce me to anyone," a high-pitched voice squeals; it reminds me of nails on a chalkboard, grating and earsplitting.

Oliver's head falls back in exasperation, and he runs his hands over his face again until they knot in his hair. "It's . . . sour."

I have to press my lips together to hold back the giggle building in my throat.

"It's not funny," he chides, but I can't help it. Exhaustion from the last couple of days is starting to take its toll, and my face splits into an ear-to-ear grin as my shoulders shake.

"It's a little funny," I tell him quietly between giggles. "Maybe we can introduce your sourdough starter to our new bookworm. I think they'd be quick friends."

With that, Oliver breaks. His face screws into an expression that speaks of his own amused disbelief at this absurd situation, and we both fall into fits of laughter. But when the chuckles eventually die out, we're left with an awkward silence filled with unanswered questions and seemingly unsolvable problems.

"So, what do we do now?" Oliver asks, and I feel as though he's asking about more than just the curse.

I shake my head. "I don't know. Grandma didn't teach us much about curses, let alone how to break them. She always emphasized staying away from them altogether. When I was younger, I thought it was just common sense; now I realize there was more to it than that. Lucy thinks our only hope is to go about things the old-fashioned way: Solve the riddle, break the curse."

His lip curls, and I can see the gears of his mind turning with thought. "My grandpa and dad taught me what they could. Shockingly enough, grandpa had a small obsession with breaking curses." A laugh bubbles out of him at that. "But my hometown didn't have much magic to speak of. Enough to learn by, but nothing like Ashwood Haven. All his lessons were more theoretical than practical."

We fall into a thoughtful lull, listening to the sourdough starter whine and moan about loneliness and manners. Oliver stares in that direction, hand on his chin, eyes distant as if reliving those old memories.

"I'll have to pull out some of my old notes, but I think I might have an idea. Can we do it tonight?"

"Oh, sure." I cock my head at him, my words flat with sarcasm. "We can do that right in the middle of the movies tonight."

He blinks at me. "What movies?"

I cross my arms over my chest, all the irritation I built up overnight flooding back. "The movies. You know, the ones you cheated your way into getting complimentary tickets to?"

A cocky grin splits his face. "Oh, yeah. Forgot about that. I won a VIP ticket to attend tonight's movie fest alongside this year's sponsor."

I roll my eyes.

Men and their egos, I swear.

"So we sneak away. Who cares?"

A blush creeps up my neck at the thought of everyone seeing Oliver and I sneak off in the dead of night. After all the shit they were giving me last night about my love life? No thanks. "I do. Everyone will think we're hooking up."

His brows tick up, and that dimple in his cheek makes an appearance, a mischievous look that says he's perfectly okay with that. That look sends my thoughts spiraling, wondering what it would be like to actually sneak off with him in the night. For him to grab my hand and lead me off into the shadows, closing the space between us and showing me what that kiss two nights ago would have felt like if we could have followed through.

But just like that, the already buzzing magic we've been keeping at bay starts to build. This whole time, we've kept distance between us, kept the conversation focused on the seriousness of this curse, but now that it's turned flirty, the magic is starting to roil. Despite knowing the consequences, it pushes my thoughts and eyes further south. Moving from his lips to the full expanse of his chest, the sleeves of his shirt hugging his arms . . . and lower. When I feel the heat of his gaze on me as well, the magic starts to grow ever more antsy, becoming a crawling sensation along my skin, warning me away as it pulls me closer.

Oliver steps closer, narrowing the space between us, but the moment is immediately ruined by a screeching wail coming from the back room.

I stumble back toward the door, allowing the heat between us to cool off and the magic to begin settling again.

"So . . ." I start, determinedly holding his gaze and refusing to let my mind wander anymore. "Sneak away from the movie tonight. Got it."

Oliver's face is blazing red as he turns away, running that hand through his hair. "Got it."

I rush out the door and back to Moonlit Pages. The moment the glass is between us, the town's magic fades away, returning to a state of happy contentment.

Chapter Sixteen

"'Til truths unfold, and masks descend,'" Oliver mutters yet again, poring over the curse as if he hasn't spent the last hour at the coffee bar reading everything we found relating to his grandfather and his family's history here in Ashwood Haven. "I mean . . . It sounds like all we have to do is figure out whatever truth it's referring to and we'll be all set."

"Easier said than done," Lucy muses as she pours sweet foam over the top of a vibrant green matcha latte. "There's no mention of a lie or a betrayal in there anywhere."

She comes around the end of the coffee bar, handing the cup to Oliver, who sits on one of the stools. He takes a sip of the matcha, and I can't look away as he uses his tongue to clean the light green foam from his lip before setting the cup down on the counter.

Oliver frowns down at the diary, reading over the curse again. "I don't think it's that simple. If it were, it'd be more of a hex or a jinx. Something easily undone with an apology and a quick reversal spell. But with the way the magic is acting, this goes way deeper than that. We have to figure out what it was that happened between our grandparents that was so hurtful neither of them could own up to it, then we might be on the right track."

I eye the open diary in his hands from where I'm kneeling on the floor, a stack of self-help books beside me. From what we've gathered over the last few days, the magic seems most upset by our immediate proximity. So long as we keep ourselves firmly planted several feet apart, with no intention of coming closer, the magic should remain a paltry hum.

"I don't see how that's possible." I mark the top book down in my inventory and reshelve it right beside the bookworm who's camped out along with us. "It's not like we can ask her . . ."

When neither of them answers, I glance up to see two identical looks of concern written across both their faces, and I know my tone was more wistful than I intended.

I shake off the weight of their worried gazes and return to the task at hand. "Oh, stop it, both of you. I'm fine."

"Clearly," Lucy mutters, that single word dripping with sarcasm.

I prickle, but I choose not to respond and, instead, scowl down at the paperback workbook in my lap, the title stamped across the front in bold letters.

Here's Your Map, Now Ask For Directions: A Beginner's Guide to Self-Love

"Well, in lieu of solving the riddle, we'll need a plan B." Oliver sets the diary aside, opting instead for his matcha. "Which reminds me, either of you know the moon phase tonight?"

My face scrunches to the side with uncertainty. Usually, I keep close track of the moon, but the past few weeks have been so busy with festival planning, decorating, and anxious worrying that I've lost track of the days.

"Half waxing," I guess, after some mental calculations, though it comes out as more of a question than a statement. I look to Lucy for help, who pulls out her phone.

"Yeah, that's right," she confirms. "Fifty-three percent, to be exact."

Oliver's eyes lift to the ceiling with his own internal figuring, bouncing back and forth as he thinks. "So, there's still a week before the full."

"Thankfully," I breathe. It's bad enough that this is all happening just days before Halloween, the day magic is at its peak. I can't even imagine if it were a full moon as well. We might as well count the town as a loss at that point and move on with our lives.

"But it's still building, and it's more than not . . ." His words are quiet as he trails off in thought. His eyes squeeze shut, and I can practically see the wheels turning in his mind, reaching back in his memory for anything that might be helpful. All of a sudden, his eyes fly open, and he points at me with renewed energy.

He begins shuffling through the notebooks, news articles, and diaries spread out across the counter until he finds one he brought from his own stash of family memorabilia. It's a thick leather-bound tome that reminds me of our own book of shadows, sitting closed and untouched on our counter since the night of the Witch's Market. Flipping through the pages, he scans each one, snapping his fingers as he tries to think.

"Do you have a stock of the basics? Sage smudgers, moon salt, the whole thing?"

I shrug, almost offended, because what kind of a question is that? "Of course, don't you?"

"I just moved," he reminds me.

"Still," I tease.

He rolls his eyes. "Bring them tonight, we'll need them."

"For what exactly?"

"A bread-breaking ritual. The whole thing started because of bad blood between families. A bread-breaking ritual might be enough to prove a renewed peace and sort of reconcile what's gone wrong, counteracting the curse." He points at Lucy. "You'll need to come too."

Lucy shoves a black sparkly fingernail into her chest. "Me? What did I do? I'm an innocent bystander in this whole thing."

Oliver gives her a flat look. "Oh, please."

"Well, I am," Lucy mumbles, crossing her arms and narrowing her eyes with a look so pointed it could be a dagger.

Oliver ignores her, which I must admit is pretty entertaining. There aren't many people willing to go toe to toe with Lucy on her best day, let alone one of her worst. It's quite a sight to watch someone so easily match her energy and put her in her place.

"We need a third to moderate the whole thing. Plus, you can build a protective barrier to keep any rebound in check if it backfires."

Lucy hums with thought, already moving on from her death stare to seriously contemplate Oliver's suggestion. I, on the other hand, am not so convinced.

Lucy glances at the book in Oliver's hands, reading over the ritual he's opened to.

"It says the ritual concludes with you each feeding the other a piece of the broken bread. I assume that means it needs to be edible, so that leaves that to Oliver."

"Rude," I grunt, but Oliver just snorts.

"I have the stuff for a loaf."

I chuckle. "Will it be sourdough?"

"That thing still won't shut up," he laments, pinching the bridge of his nose between thumb and forefinger. "At least I won't have to worry about it tomorrow."

"What's happening tomorrow? Aside from the haunted houses."

"I was thinking I'd open the doors for the night and hand out samples. Chocolate-orange cookies, chai apple cupcakes . . ."

Lucy perks up at the sound of that. "Apple fritters?"

Oliver shoots her a look out of the corner of his eye that suggests she's already hit her fritter limit for the week, which earns him a pout that he promptly ignores.

"Anyway, since it's a night of haunted houses and ghost tours, I figured no one would notice a whining, screeching sourdough starter. That gives me one more day to figure out what to do with the damn thing." He lets out a heavy sigh before returning to the subject at hand. "So, bread-breaking ritual. What do you think?"

"I don't know." I purse my lips in thought as I count another shelf of self-help books, marking the numbers on a pad of paper. "Something about it feels wrong. I'm not saying it's necessarily a bad idea, but it doesn't seem like enough."

"It'd be more powerful than what we tried. More intentional," Lucy offers.

"That's what worries me. Not only is Halloween in two days, but we're trying a more straightforward approach. Do you realize how badly that could backfire?"

"That's what the barrier is for," Oliver reminds me.

"Besides, the whole town will be gathered in the square for movie night. That means we have the place to ourselves, and if something does go spectacularly wrong, maybe no one will notice." Lucy gives a happy little wiggle as she takes her first sip of her pumpkin-spiced latte, her red curls brushing her shoulders.

I give her a flat glare, shifting my gaze to the worm sitting on the shelf beside me.

"I think this town could use a bit more variety," our new friend informs us, raising its little nose in the air. "It is the spice of life, after all, and you all seem to be very speciesist."

I roll my eyes until they land on Lucy once again, who at least has the decency to grimace.

"Point taken," she mutters as she takes another sip.

If the last few days have taught us anything, it's that the magic is being anything but subtle. At this rate, I wouldn't even be surprised if our next punishment was for the characters on the big screen to step right onto the streets of Ashwood Haven and start terrorizing townspeople; how very Frankenstein.

The movie, not the book.

I turn my attention back to the bookworm. "If a customer comes in here, you'd better hide."

"Just proving my point," it declares.

I run my hands over my face, digging the heels of my palms into my eyes. Between running the bookstore, dealing with magical outbursts, and the worst of them all, hosting the festival, I'm absolutely exhausted. I can handle everything else, but hosting duties have drained my social battery down to its dregs, and I can tell I'm about to snap. All the attention, socializing, and responsibilities are wearing me down day by day, and I keep reminding myself that

Grandma did this well into her sixties. Hell, she would have done it from her deathbed if given the choice.

If she can do it, so can I . . . I just need to figure out how she did it.

I can feel both Lucy and Oliver's eyes on me, and when I look their way, the concerned expressions on their faces make me want to cave in on myself harder.

"I'm fine," I grit through clenched teeth, snapping at the pair of them.

The two exchange a meaningful look, and I'm starting to think that maybe I don't like seeing them together after all.

"If you have something to say, then say it," I snap once more, giving in to the exhaustion wearing on my bones.

Lucy quirks an eyebrow at me, and an icy mask starts to slip across her face.

So much tension builds between us that even Oliver starts to squirm on his stool, looking a lot like someone who's been caught in the middle of something they didn't mean to walk in on.

"Fine," Lucy bites back, balancing her drink on her criss-crossed legs, her spine so straight it could be made of steel. "You aren't Grandma."

"What does that mean?"

"It means you're bending over backward to prove to this whole town that you can fill her shoes, when—in reality—you're hating every second. You don't owe them anything, especially not your sanity. I think you'd be better off hiding here for the rest of the festival and telling them all to screw themselves. Or better yet, let me do it for you."

I narrow my eyes at her, refusing to show the way her words spear me right through the chest.

"If you hate this town so much, then why are you still here?" I spit at her, and I can tell by the way her gaze darkens that the words hit their mark. "Oh, that's right! Because—"

"Amelia," she cuts me off, her tone slicing across my skin like a dried corn stalk leaf. "I love you. Don't say things you don't mean."

I promptly shut my mouth so hard my teeth clack, holding back the rest of my sentence. I take a moment, running my hands through my black hair and my nails across my scalp as I breathe deep. A few heartbeats later, I'm drained of all my fight.

"I'm sorry," I whisper, just loud enough for her to hear.

The worm peeks around the edge of a book, pointedly turning its attention on Lucy. "Why haven't you left?"

With a flick of her hand, Lucy sends the book in my lap back onto the shelf, hiding the worm from view and forcing it back to wherever it goes during the day.

The three of us fall into a heavy silence, punctuated by Lucy taking a long, loud sip of her drink. After what feels like an eternity, Oliver clears his throat and straightens on his stool, using his feet to push against the bottom rung and twist back and forth like a little kid who can't sit still.

"So . . ." he starts, trying and failing to sound casual. "Where should this all take place?"

"Where should what take place?" I ask, keeping my tone as friendly as possible.

"The bread-breaking ritual."

"I don't know," I admit after a moment.

Lucy hums with thought, swirling her hand over the top of her cup to slowly stir the contents. "Why not the woods?"

"Isn't that a little too . . . horror movie? Two girls wandering off into the forest on the edge of town with a strange man they met a few days ago?"

Oliver's brows furrow with exaggerated offense, holding a hand to his chest like a damsel in an old-timey movie.

"Maybe a little," Lucy admits.

"Crying a little inside over here." Oliver sulks, though neither of us pays him much attention.

"But it's within the bounds of the magic and far enough from the town square that maybe the rebound from a failed attempt won't cause any chaos."

I contemplate the suggestion. "Okay, that's fair."

"So, it's settled then? I'll meet you two tonight after you sneak away from the movies."

"Do I get a say?" Oliver glances between us and waves a forlorn hand in the air to get our attention.

Lucy and I look at each other for a brief moment before returning our attention to him.

"No," we say in unison.

Oliver takes a long sip of his matcha before setting the half-empty cup on the counter. "I get the feeling I'm going to need a lot more caffeine to keep up with the two of you."

Chapter Seventeen

The moment hot, buttery popcorn hits my tongue, I have to suppress a moan, savoring the salty crunch. I side-eye the bowl of cheese-topped chili and the bag of miniature fried donuts, piled high with cinnamon sugar, balanced in Oliver's hands. "I can't believe you aren't getting popcorn. I think that's a sin or something."

"I like to switch it up sometimes." He lifts the bag to his mouth, grabs the topmost donut with his teeth, and draws the whole thing into his mouth.

"But it's a movie night. By definition, that requires the consumption of popcorn. And none of that air-popped healthy stuff either." I pick a grease-drenched puff off the top of my massive bag, popping it between my lips for emphasis. "It needs to be the most heart-stopping, butter-drenched, salt-laden perfection you've ever eaten."

Oliver scowls down at my bright yellow snack, glistening in the lights of the nearest food truck, hung with fairy lights and glowing pumpkin ornaments.

"That's not even real butter."

I raise an eyebrow at him before turning my attention to my popcorn, inspecting one of the top kernels closely. "How can you tell?"

He snorts. "I come from a long line of bakers who make everything from scratch. Real sugar, real fruit, real butter. I can smell the difference from a mile away."

He grabs another donut from his bag with his teeth, tipping his head back to scarf it down in one gulp.

"Uh-huh . . . and how's your sugar dough fried in dirty oil?"

"Perfection." He grins.

I roll my eyes at him and shake my head to hide my grin. We meander through the food trucks lined up along Main Street, doing our best not to bump into the crowd gathered in the middle. There's everything from classic fair foods to quirky, unusual trucks that have come from all over the East Coast.

Right next to a corndog truck is one selling custom ice cream sandwiches, the scent of freshly baked cookies mixing with the salty, greasy smell of cheap hot dogs. Then, just like that, there's a ramen truck advertising everything from spicy miso ramen to ramen tacos next to it. The longest line, though, is for the gourmet grilled cheese truck, which I have to admit was very tempting.

Oliver leans closer until his breath brushes against the tip of my ear. "How were things after I left?"

In the small space between us, the magic flares. Up until now, it's been idly buzzing around us like an annoying mosquito, watching and waiting for its chance to take its bite, but the sudden proximity shift grabs its attention, waiting for us to get too close.

I sigh, leaning away, because I don't have to ask to know what he's referring to. Even after he left, the tension between Lucy and me hung in the air. As lifelong friends who'd been working together for damn near a decade, we've had our fair share of fights. Still, each one wore on me as if it were the first time.

"If I say fine, will you believe me?"

"No."

Figures.

We come to the end of the food trucks, taking in a much-needed breath of fresh air, free of mouthwatering scents, and I scan the area: There's a massive screen constructed before the town gazebo, rows and rows of folding chairs lined up before it.

We stand there for a long time, swaying back and forth as I inspect my popcorn with an intensity that suggests they might come alive and start swarming like spiders. Given the way things have gone this week, that isn't all that unlikely.

Oliver breaks the silence first. "She's right, you know."

"Traitor." I glower at him from beneath my lashes, doing my best impression of a scathing look, but the way he smiles tells me I come off more like a feisty kitten than a lion.

"Can I be honest?" he asks. I don't answer, but I don't walk away either, and he takes that as enough consent to keep going. "From what I've noticed, you're hiding behind a pretty transparent mask. I don't know you that well, but even I can tell you're hating this whole 'host' thing. You run a successful, well-respected business, and it's clear this whole town loves you the way you are. There are so many other ways you could be contributing to this festival to make it equally as memorable as any other year, so why are you trying to be something you're not?"

I roll back and forth on my feet, holding my popcorn bag close. "You don't get it. No one does," I reply softly.

Oliver doesn't respond, just stands there watching me, patiently waiting for me to find the words.

"It's not about me."

"Then who is it about? The town? The festival? Because I promise, they'll survive."

"No, it's . . ." My jaw clenches as I struggle to find the right words. To speak aloud all the things I've been keeping to myself. "It's about Grandma."

"But you're not—"

"I know, I'm not Grandma," I bite out, cutting him off before he can say what I know is coming. "I'm not trying to *be* her. I could never be her, but she was my everything. My best friend—and my role model. She was everything I *wanted* to be when I grew up, and then one day she was just . . . gone. Yes, her health had been declining for a few years, but I still wasn't ready. Because the day she found out we would be hosting this year, her face lit up. For the first time in months, that spark was back, and she'd been so excited. We started planning that day. Talking about all the things we wanted to contribute, how we'd decorate the store, and all the little bits of magic we'd infuse into the celebration to make it all that much more special."

Tears dance on my lashes as I remember it all, the memories barreling through me like a wrecking ball determined to make me collapse beneath its weight.

"I'm not trying to *be* Grandma," I repeat. "I'm just trying to live my life in a way that would make her proud. Hosting a successful Halloween . . ." I gesture to the square around us. To the smiling, laughing, chatting festivalgoers, and all the decorations I'd helped fund. "This would have meant the world to her."

A single tear slides down my cheek, and I wipe at it with the heel of my hand. Oliver reaches for me and then freezes, his hand hanging in midair before clenching his fist and letting it fall to his side, remembering that the magic reacts most when we touch.

"Amelia!" The screech scares me half to death, making me jump and nearly spill my popcorn everywhere.

I spin to find Stacy storming toward me, clipboard in hand.

"There you are!"

"Here I am," I breathe, trying my best not to sound so despondent about that fact. Before she gets too close, I swipe at my cheeks, forcing away any remaining tears and splitting my face with a smile that doesn't reach my eyes.

Thankfully, Stacy is too focused on her timetable to notice. "I need you pronto. All the cooking competition winners are waiting for you in the VIP section. Well"—she glances at Oliver, giving him the dirtiest stink eye I've ever seen from her, and I almost snort at his berated expression—"almost all of them."

"I'm headed there now," I assure her, plastering on a cordial smile. "Just show me where to sit."

With a snap of her fingers, she gestures for me to follow, leading Oliver and me through the gate toward a roped-off table at the center of the makeshift theater seating. Stacy wasn't joking; all the seats are taken, all except for two. One in the very center, which I sadly assume is my seat, and one at the very end. She herds me toward the center seat while rambling about the importance of punctuality.

I plop into my seat, holding my bag of popcorn close, and give Ellie a small, friendly smile. She wiggles her fingers in greeting as she slurps her noodles, the ramen truck logo printed on the side of the bowl.

I glance down at the end as Oliver takes his seat next to Charissa, who unsurprisingly won the cocktail/mocktail category last night. They shake hands, and Oliver smoothly slips into a charismatic conversation with her that sends her into a flurry of animated hand movements, probably talking about her latest microbrew.

The sight of him fitting in so effortlessly here warms my heart. If you don't count stepping on Stacy's punctual toes, of course, but even the oldest residents of Ashwood Haven can't avoid that. From what he's shared, it seems like he could really use a place to call home, somewhere he belongs and can be himself without the pressures of family or his past catching up to him. The bright, easy smile stretching across his face, the dimple forming at the corner, tells me he feels it too—that sense that he's meant to be here, meant to run the bakery.

Maybe . . . meant to find me.

Sadness takes hold of my heart because what if the magic runs him out of town the same way it did his grandfather . . . and if it does, it'll all be my fault. Or, more specifically, Grandma's fault.

I'm reminded that if we are destined to find each other, it isn't for any good reason. If anything, we've been pushed together so I can ruin his life.

"Do you know what's showing tonight?" Ellie inquires, drawing my attention.

I turn to her, pulling myself out of my spiral long enough to remember the incredibly detailed email Stacy sent me regarding every second of the week-long festival.

"Um, the family movie is Halloween Town, and the not-so-family movie is . . . Saw. I think."

Ellie's face screws up with distaste. "Yeah, I'll be skipping that one."

I chuckle. "Not a Saw fan?"

"I work for the fire department. I've seen more than my fair share of wreckage and ruined bodies. What do you think?" She shivers and jumps, as if the very thought of it makes her skin crawl.

The smile I give her in return is small, but after the week I've had, it's the best I can muster. It's not that I don't like Ellie. In fact, she's one of my favorite people in town. She's strong, bubbly, and one of the most independent people I've ever met, without making me feel like I'm lesser for not being that way myself. But talking to her is still a form of socialization, and I'm just . . . over it.

Thankfully, before I'm forced to make any more small talk, the lights around the square dim, and the opening music of Halloween Town blares from the speakers. I settle into my folding chair, nodding my head to the jazzy tune.

As the movie plays, I can't help but occasionally sneak a peek over at Oliver at the end of the table. The whole time, he's completely absorbed in the film, eating spoonfuls of his chili and the occasional cinnamon sugar donut. But when I catch him mouthing the words to Dylan's scathing review of Halloween and Marnie's iconic "Halloween is cool" rebuttal, complete with a sassy head bob and everything, I practically swoon. I become very aware of the way the colors from the movie screen cast shadows across his face, highlighting the line of his jaw and the thick column of his neck.

My breath hitches as something stirs deep in my belly, in time for the magic to start stirring as well. It bubbles between us, each pop sending sparks through the air, and I tear my eyes away from his as Oliver meets my gaze. Instead, I direct my attention back to the movie and shove a palm full of popcorn into my mouth, swallowing it down along with my feelings that need to stay right where they are.

A brisk breeze blows through the crowd, cutting through my jacket and making me shiver. Goose bumps rise along my skin until warmth creeps through the fabric, swaddling me like a heated blanket on a cold winter night. The warmth is accompanied by a subtle sizzle of magic, and I glance at Oliver out of the corner of my eye, who's covering quiet words with a fake cough.

This time, he doesn't look my way, pointedly focusing on the movie, but his small knowing smile tells me he can feel my eyes on him and is refusing to acknowledge my scolding look. He knows he shouldn't be doing something as stupid as using magic two nights before Halloween to bring me comfort, especially not with all these people around.

But I'd be lying if I said it didn't make me want to start kicking my feet and twirling my hair like a middle school girl talking to her crush in the hallway. It feels so good to have someone take care of me without asking first if I'm okay, which has quickly become my least favorite question in the world. To have someone notice my discomfort and take the initiative, rather than trying to convince me to do it myself. So, I nuzzle down further into my jacket, allowing myself to enjoy the warmth and the attention while I can. So long as the magic doesn't see this small act as reason enough to respond, I might as well enjoy it.

About the time the kids find their way to Halloween Town and start exploring, I straighten in my chair and turn to Ellie. She gives me a questioning glance, noticing me scooting away from the table.

"Water," I whisper, and she nods, happily returning her attention to the movie.

Without looking back, I make my way down the center aisle of the seats and back toward the long line of food trucks. The lines have died down considerably now that the movie has started, but there are still a few people lingering here and there, grabbing a quick bite or drink. I approach a hot chocolate truck near the end, one far enough in that it's not visible from the outdoor theater. The agreed meeting point for Oliver and me before we sneak off to find Lucy.

With a finger to my chin, I study the menu, trying to appear as if I can't decide between the spiced Mexican hot chocolate or the mega chocolate. The conglomeration comes with so many different toppings and drizzles that the never-ending list takes up four lines on the board. Just the thought of it makes my stomach roil, and yet . . . I'm intrigued.

I stand there so long that the girl behind the cash register starts to eye me warily.

"Do you have any questions?" The way she asks it sounds as if she'd rather be asking if I'm going to order in this lifetime or the next.

"Um, yes . . ." My words trail off as I try to think of something to ask, as I scan the line of trucks, searching for a large form to come save me from this awkward interaction. "Are your . . . er, actually, was your Mexican hot chocolate made in Mexico?"

When the stunned woman in the truck blinks at me, I play back what I just said, and I decide it is, in fact, possible to die of humiliation. I stare at her open-mouthed, trying to decide if I should take the question back or if that would look even worse.

"We make all of our hot chocolates in the truck, ma'am," the woman eventually answers.

I repress a sigh at myself. "Of course you do . . . obviously. Can I just get—Oh, crap!"

Around the corner of the food truck hall comes Stacy, staring at that damned clipboard.

"Maybe next time!" I squeak at the hot chocolate lady, and before I can tell if the look on her face is relief that she doesn't have to answer any more questions or concern for my mental state, I dart between trucks. I trip over lines of extension cords laid out across the ground, too busy checking over my shoulder to make sure the coordinator hasn't seen me shirking my hostess duties.

I make a sharp turn, veering away from the trucks and toward town hall. There's a large statue of a man sitting atop a horse that looks out over the square from a distance. Its base is so wide that three people could stand shoulder to shoulder behind it, and a person sitting in the gazebo wouldn't even know they're there. I dart behind it, and after a moment, I peek around the corner to make sure an angry wedding coordinator hasn't followed me.

"Did she see you?"

I jump, clamping a hand over my mouth to suppress a scream when I turn and find Oliver hovering over my shoulder.

"Don't do that!" I press a palm to my chest to ease my racing heart, but he just laughs, his shoulders shaking with amusement.

Adrenaline rushes through my veins, causing a burst of giggles that make me sound like a sixteen-year-old sneaking off at night with her crush. As opposed to a grown woman, who has every right to leave a movie night if she wants to. I feel like I'm back in high school, reminded of the time Lucy talked me into cutting class. This time, I won't spend the whole time so anxious about the homework assignment I'd be missing that I can't enjoy a minute of it.

The whole thing feels a bit ludicrous, and I realize how immature I'm being. Sneaking off to avoid Stacy, like an overbearing parent. I'm nearly thirty, not a teenager. But I have to admit . . . I'm having fun. For the first time during this event, I'm actually enjoying myself and getting a taste of that mischievous side everyone should experience during Halloween. I like the way Oliver brings that out in me and the way he feels like an escape from my socialization duties, rather than just another person to check off my list.

"Come on." I smile at him, waving for him to follow me after one last look to make sure the coast is clear. "Lucy's waiting."

Chapter Eighteen

Once we get on the now-abandoned path of the lantern walk from a couple of nights ago, it doesn't take long to find Lucy in the woods. She's set up a circle of thick sticks and fist-sized rocks, creating a boundary for us to work within. On a nearby boulder, she sits cross-legged, as per usual, playing on her phone as if she isn't randomly hanging out in the middle of the woods two nights before Halloween. The arms of her fuzzy checkered coat lay limp by her side, her arms tucked into the body so that the glow from her phone lights up her face through the neck hole. Around the circle, she's set up fake candles, which flicker and dance on a phantom breeze.

"What witch uses fake candles?" Oliver eyes the circle with a mix of scrutiny and amusement.

"I'm not trying to start a forest fire," Lucy retorts. "Besides, it's the thought that counts."

"That's not . . ." Oliver starts, then he simply shakes his head.

"Whatever. The candles aren't what's important here. Did you bring the rest?"

"Of course." Reluctantly, Lucy gets to her feet and grabs a cardboard box that had previously been sitting on the ground beside the boulder and starts laying out the contents on a nearby downed tree. Including, but not limited to, Oliver's own book of shadows, since we still can't trust our own.

Oliver takes the book and flips through it until he finds the page he's looking for and lays the book flat against the boulder before turning to me.

"Ready?" he asks.

I shake my head, warily eyeing the circle the way a bug might a Venus flytrap. "No."

"Good!" Lucy claps her hands together before bouncing on her toes and shaking out her arms. "Let's get this over with. It's freezing—and I'm hungry. Some of us haven't had a chance to visit Food Truck Alley yet."

I sigh. Just as I know I have to host the festival, I also know I need to do this. If we wait even one more day, the magic might get so out of hand that we can't handle it anymore. If we wait too long and let Halloween pass, there might not be enough magical oomph to do anything at all. That doesn't mean I'm not dreading it, though . . . Something deep in my gut is telling me this is a bad idea. That the consequences are something we aren't prepared to handle. But what choice do we have?

So, I step into the circle with Oliver and we face each other, waiting for Lucy to get things started.

Lucy picks up a smudge stick, lights it with a match to let it burn briefly, then blows it out, allowing the smoke to swirl in the cool air. With slow, methodical movements, she begins painting X's through the air along the border of our circle; the scent of white sage, lavender, and rosemary grows stronger with each pass.

Despite the ever-buzzing magic between Oliver and me, I feel lighter with each swipe of the smudger. It might not be visible, but I can sense the barrier building around us, cutting us off from the rest of the forest. The click and rhythmic song of nighttime bugs becomes deadened background noise, and even the crunch beneath Lucy's boots takes on a muted quality, as though there's a thick blanket between us and the world.

When the barrier is complete, Lucy sets the smudge stick aside, somewhere it can't cause any further problems, and picks up the cloth-wrapped loaf of bread Oliver dropped off at the bookstore earlier. She quickly reads over the ritual again before coming to stand within the boundaries of our circle. With a hand on both the top and the bottom of the rounded loaf, she holds it out between us and clears her throat.

"Do you come to this circle with an open mind and agreeable heart?" Her emerald eyes take on a serious edge, darkening until the clover green is almost black.

"I come to heal what has been wronged," I tell her, repeating the line I memorized earlier.

She asks the same of Oliver, who gives the same answer in return.

Around us, the magic starts to crackle like static, and I can't tell if it's happy we are trying to find peace, or if it's angry at yet another attempt to bypass what it was originally promised: *The truth*. Whatever it is.

With her top hand, Lucy unwraps the loaf of bread, revealing a perfectly browned top, sprinkled with thyme and salt. Oliver and I each grab our respective sides of the bread, and it crackles in our hands, the crust crisp atop a pliant center.

Lucy glances back at the book once more before closing her eyes, taking a deep breath to center herself, to start the spell in full. "Let bread be broken, not bonds of hate. Let peace fill what once held weight. From grain to grace, from crust to core, we close this path of ancient war."

Despite the melodic cadence of Lucy's words, the rhyme hangs heavy around us. It becomes a rope wrapping tighter and tighter with each sentence, the magic pressing closer until it becomes hard to breathe.

"Break the bread, formed by your own hands. Kneaded from memory and baked with intent," she commands, her voice taking on a deep raspy edge.

My fingers break through the crust of the bread, digging into the soft center, and the magic around us begins to swarm with furious energy. It lifts our hair on a phantom wind, a tornado whipping and whirling. Oliver and I lock eyes, my own uncertainty reflected in his pale gaze.

"Break the bread!" Lucy commands, her words rising above the tunnel of chaos we're standing at the center of.

Without another moment's hesitation, I pull. The loaf of bread tears in two, and the magic explodes.

The three of us are thrown back and crash against the barrier. The magic ping-pongs off the barrier, violently ricocheting around as it searches for a way out. I shield my head with my hands, burying my face in the dirt. A scream rakes against my throat, and my whole body trembles as the magic reaches its peak, pounding against the barrier. I pull my elbows in closer, trying to curl into a fetal position, and catch the corner of one of the wrist-thick sticks forming the boundary of our circle.

The branch shifts and the magic whooshes out in a gust of wind, dissipating into the night.

Eventually, I start to sit up and realize I'm still clutching my half of the loaf in my hand. Only now, the perfectly baked round of bread is nothing more than a dense ball of carbs.

I throw it to the ground like it suddenly became diseased and run my hands through my hair, pulling at the roots.

After a long, long silence, Lucy pushes a heavy breath through tight lips. "Well, that didn't work."

My hands fall, my elbows resting on my knees as I send her a deadpan glare. "You think? Really?"

"Just an observation," she snarls, fluffing out her red curls and pulling a twig from her hair with a sneer.

"What the hell kind of magic do you guys have here?" Oliver stammered, more to himself than to us.

"The barrier broke. You don't think the magic is going to cause any trouble, do you?" I don't direct the question to anyone in particular.

"Oh, I hope not," Oliver mumbles, running his hands over his face.

"No, I don't think so," Lucy answers, glancing around the woods. "That was a pretty serious whirlwind, and nothing outside the circle seems disturbed."

We all sit there for a while, catching our breath and listening to the sounds of the forest return.

"So what do we do now?" Oliver prods, breaking the silence.

My brows fly so high they practically reach my hairline. "You want to try again?"

"I'm supposed to be opening a new business in two days, and I don't want to get run out of town like my papa."

"That's fair." I moan into my hands, wanting nothing more than to curl up into a ball and give up. This whole thing is such a mess. Not only is the biggest money maker of the year at risk, but so is Oliver's entire livelihood. Starting a new business is expensive, and he gave up his entire life to take this risk. Giving up isn't an option, but I don't know what else to do.

"I don't think we have any more options," Lucy asserts, pulling her knees to her chest. "There's only one way we're going to break this thing once and for all."

"The old-fashioned way," I whine.

She nods. "We have to figure out what the curse wants. We have to solve the riddle. No more trying to work around it."

Oliver nods as well. "Agreed."

"Okay," I whine again. "Does anyone remember it?"

"'Til truths unfold, and masks descend. Two wounded souls, their stories lend," Lucy repeats, reciting the curse verbatim without hesitation.

I quirk a questioning brow at her.

She shrugs. "I've read it enough over the last few days I've got it memorized."

I decide not to question her any further, grateful that she knows the curse at all, saving us the time of having to return to the store to find it.

"The only thing I can think is that the curse just wants honesty," Oliver offers, wrapping his arms around his knees.

"But what about?" I plead, desperate to find a solution to this mess.

Oliver's brows start twitching, his eyes narrowing with confusion as he sniffs the air. He looks like a dog walking by a barbecue, his nose bouncing up and down.

"Are you having a stroke?" Lucy sneers, leaning away from him like he's about to snap and lose his mind.

"Do you guys smell . . ." He sniffs again. "Fake butter?"

"Like the popcorn?" I ask.

Oliver's expression falls, a look of horror washing over his face. "Exactly like the popcorn."

It takes a moment for his words to sink in, and then we all jump to our feet, sprinting headlong toward Main Square.

Chapter Nineteen

Stumbling into the town square to find it flooded with a mountain of popcorn was not on my Halloween bingo card, and yet . . . here we are. There's enough popcorn in the middle of town to feed an army of moviegoers *and* their rivals. In fact, this could feed every dragon in the last fantasy world I read about, along with their riders. It's a comical amount of fluffy white kernels that are still piling up as we arrive. The smell is honestly heavenly if you ask me, but the disgusted look on Oliver's face suggests he thinks otherwise.

Stacy is impossible to miss, screeching like a banshee and waving that damn clipboard in the air.

"Where is she?!" Stacy yells at anyone who will listen; poor Don is standing nearby, taking the brunt of her wrath.

I groan because I know instantly who *she* is, and I would give anything not to be her.

"Maybe she's looking for me?" Lucy offers, her face screwed up with a mix of apprehension and sympathy.

Stacy's blazing eyes land on me, and I feel like a red flag in a bull fight.

"I don't think so," I groan. "Why don't you head back to the store? I'll meet you there shortly."

Lucy side-eyes Stacy, storming toward us with Don close on her heels. "You sure?"

"I'll stay with her," Oliver offers, stepping closer.

"That's what I'm worried about," Lucy grumbles under her breath before giving me another sympathetic look and heading toward Moonlit Pages.

"I have been looking everywhere for you!" Stacy points at me with her clipboard, wielding it like a dagger she fully intends to plunge through my heart.

I stutter, looking for some reasonable excuse as to why I never returned. I glance at the movie screen, the climax building to a head as Marnie and her family start confronting Kalabar, and not for the first time in my life, I find myself envious of fictional characters. Oh, what I wouldn't give to be able to say a spell and make everything better. Because trust me, I've been trying.

"There was an issue at the store," Oliver jumps in, nudging me with his elbow.

"Yeah, Marilyn called and needed help," I finished, hoping that would be enough of an explanation.

"Oh no, because Ellie told me you went to get some water and never came back, so I *went* to the store," Stacy yells, pointing down the street toward Moonlit Pages with an accusatory finger. "Marilyn told me she hasn't seen you all night. But since Oliver wasn't at the movie either, I thought perhaps you were at the bakery."

"Oh no," Oliver breathes.

"And what I heard coming from that bakery, you're lucky I

didn't break down that door! Screeching and whining and the most horrific singing I'd ever heard. I almost called the cops!"

I glance at Oliver, stammering through an explanation. "That was just . . . a Halloween tape, right?"

Oliver points at me, releasing a relieved breath. "Yes! Exactly. Just getting in the spirit of things."

Don eyes Oliver, suspicion heavy in his eyes, but he stays quiet for now, taking everything in.

"And what's this?!" Stacy throws a hand toward the ever-growing mountain of popcorn.

"Psh. That . . . wasn't me." I force a laugh through my teeth, hoping to sound amused by such an innocent prank, but instead, I sound guilty.

Stacy's eyes narrow, not buying it for a second. "You've been causing trouble all week, but *this* is too much. We're supposed to have a whole other movie after this, and your little prank has taken over half the seats! Do you understand how much time and money go into these events?"

Tears line my eyes as I take her admonishments one at a time, unable to find the words to fight back. There's nothing I can say that will change her mind. Nothing I can do to make this better. What's worse is that it *is* all my fault; it was my grandmother who placed the curse. It's *my* proximity to Oliver that's causing all these problems. If I had kept my distance the moment I realized what was going on, none of this would be happening.

"Back off, okay?" Oliver bites back, shielding me from Stacy with a thick muscled arm. "Amelia's been killing herself to host this damn thing, and you have no reason to think she caused any of this."

"You're right," Don booms, crossing his arms over his chest.

"Amelia has been a stand-up citizen of this community for many years. So let me ask you, where did you run off to during the movie, Oliver?"

Oliver's mouth falls open, but before he can stumble through some excuse, another much smaller voice nearby catches my attention.

"Mommy, what monster is that?" Nearby, a child tugs on his mother's arm, pointing to the movie screen that no one seems to be watching anymore.

I give the screen a cursory glance before turning back to the conversation at hand, and then I do a double-take.

Saw, the murderous little puppet on a tricycle, is peddling his way through the middle of the Halloween Town climax. Panic makes it impossible for me to tear my eyes from the screen as I frantically reach out, trying to get the coordinator's attention.

"Stace," I rasp.

"Don't try to change the subject," she seethes, ignoring my frenzied movements.

"Stacy," I try again, just as the Saw puppet stops in the middle of the screen, his head turning back and forth, his mouth robotically moving up and down.

"Do you want to play a game?"

"Stacy!" I screech, taking her shoulder and spinning her to look at the screen.

Her eyes nearly pop out of her head as the puppet begins laughing maniacally. Around us, parents start shrieking, grabbing their children, and turning them away from the screen. Those who are old enough to understand what's happening but have no innocent eyes to protect stare openly at the new ending that Ashwood Haven's magic gives this childhood favorite. Before Saw can start explaining the rules of the game, Stacy has her radio out and is sprinting toward the movie projector.

"Turn it off! Turn it off!"

Blood splatters across a costume-clad extra in the movie mere seconds before the screen goes black, and Main Square goes unnervingly quiet.

A mountain of popcorn? Innocent fun. A prank that annoys no one except the event organizer? Whatever. But messing with a family-friendly movie to somehow insert a murderous, sadistic puppet to start violently killing off cutely dressed characters? There's no coming back from that. Another few seconds, and the entire festival would have been ruined—and Ashwood Haven's reputation stained forever.

No parent would ever bring their kids back to an event that traumatized them, and families are the main supporters of this event. It's always been meant as good, clean fun with a few adult themes added in for good measure. Alcoholic drinks and R-rated films after the kid-friendly ones, but graphically torturing people in a family film is too far.

Don turns back to Oliver and I at an agonizingly slow pace, puffing out his chest as he does. When I look up at him, I expect to find his scathing gaze boring into me, but instead, he only has eyes for Oliver.

He thoughtfully runs his thumb and forefinger over his mustache before placing his hands on his hips. Indignation emanates from him in churning waves that make me want to shrink away. Don has always been a larger-than-life man, both in physical size and personality. With a booming voice and a commanding presence wherever he goes, it's hard to see him as anything else. That said, I've always viewed him as a giant teddy bear—a fatherlike figure who cares for the entire town as if we're all his children. And like any good father, it's not the anger that's scary . . . it's the disappointment.

Right now, Don's disappointment is a palpable thing in the air.

"Oliver, boy, I told you when you came to town that as long as you ran an honest business and stayed out of trouble, you'd be welcome here. You say you aren't involved in all of this, but let's be honest: Things aren't looking very good."

"I swear," Oliver starts, "I had nothing to do with—"

Don silences him with a wave of his hand. "This is the most important event of the year for Ashwood Haven. Now, I understand you're new, and that might not mean much to you, but it means a great deal to me. I don't think . . ." He pauses, weighing his words before continuing. "I don't think this is the right time for you to be opening a business in the middle of town."

Oliver's eyes go wide, and I can sense his building panic. "Don, I swear I had *nothing* to do with this. I don't even know how someone would merge two movies like that. I have inventory coming in tomorrow. Everything is ready. You can't just cancel my opening."

"Not cancel," Don clarifies. "Delayed a little while. We can discuss things further after Halloween is over, but I'm thinking a week or two should be sufficient."

"You have no right—"

Don turns and walks away, leaving us to watch his retreating form with slack jaws and lost hope.

Delaying the opening, in and of itself, isn't the end of the world, but the implications of it are massive. The magic is working; it's doing exactly what it set out to do. If we don't find a way to break this curse, this delay could very well turn into a permanent thing, and Oliver could lose his business before it's even open.

"You don't have to do it," I tell Oliver, trying to find my resolve. "Legally, he can't stop you. Not two days before opening."

Oliver's face falls, his shoulders curling in on themselves, making him smaller by the second. "You're right. I could just stick with my initial plan and start my business off on the wrong foot with the entire town."

I shake my head, trying to sound determined, but only coming across half-hearted. "Don's opinion isn't the only one that matters . . ."

My words trail off when Oliver's heartbroken gaze meets mine, because we both know I'm lying through my teeth. Don's opinion isn't the only one that counts, but anyone who sets foot in Ashwood Haven can tell this is a tight-knit community that stands by each other. If someone is marked as troublesome by someone as influential as Don, they don't even stand a chance. Oliver can either take Don's heavy-handed advice to heart, or he can count on closing the doors to his bakery before the year is out.

Just like his grandpa.

Chapter Twenty

The bell over the front door of Moonlit Pages chimes merrily as another group shuffles into the shop.

"Next on our tour of historic Ashwood Haven, we have the longest-running shop on Main Street: Moonlit Pages. This bookstore, passed down through generations of the Nova family, was founded in . . ." The tour guide delves into their practiced speech that I've heard hundreds of times. Tonight, Ashwood Haven is one giant haunted house and ghost tour, with creepily dressed actors roaming the town, popping out of shadowed corners at people wandering from one decked-out building to the next. This tour guide is no different, dressed in a long black cape, top hat, and button-down vest, adorned with chains and pocket watches galore. He carries an old metal lamp, lit by a battery-powered candle, complete with flickering false flame.

Moonlit Pages is a stop on the ghost tour every year—a favorite among local historians given its age and our ability to make it feel truly haunted and mystical. Given the theme of the night, neither

Lucy nor I bother to rein in Ashwood Haven's magic. Rather, this is the one night of the year we encourage it to run free.

Books drift around the store, able to wander wherever they please. New this year is the fact that they now talk, much to my dismay, but it adds to the mystical, magical atmosphere of the night. Fake candles and twinkle lights cast a warm glow over the shop, and self-sweeping brooms enhance the spooky vibe. We even let the bookworm out for the evening so they can delight shoppers and spectators alike with their not-safe-for-work recommendations and their ability to recite passages with explicit detail.

Usually, I'd dress to impress in a black and purple dress adorned with glittering spiderwebs and printed skulls, finished with a pointed-brimmed hat to complete the witchy look.

This year, though . . . I didn't have the heart.

Instead, I hide from the masses crowded between shelves from behind the register, perched on my stool in the corner as far as I can get. Since tonight's event spans all of downtown Ashwood Haven, I have no hosting duties and was instead instructed to stay in the shop, which will already see the majority of the festival attendees.

A romance novel rests open on my knees, its pages flipping of their own accord even though I stopped paying attention long ago. I had hoped it would distract me from everything that's gone wrong this week and give me hope that things would get better. If not between Oliver and me, then at least for him on his own. At least, that's what happily-ever-after love stories usually do. But so far, it's only succeeded in making me more miserable.

I pull my sleeves down over my hands, my fingers absently finding the cuff and rubbing it between my thumb and forefinger in a comforting, rhythmic motion. The coping mechanism doesn't lessen the heaviness in my chest or lift the anchors that seem to be hanging from my limbs, drowning me in a turbulent sea of my own thoughts.

For what seems like the hundredth time tonight, my eyes find the front window. Across the street, businesses are alight with strobe lights and eerie music. Even from here, I can make out the occasional delighted scream of those navigating one of the haunted houses, the roar of chainless-chainsaws coming to life every few minutes, closely followed by maniacal laughter.

To the left is a clothing boutique whose upper two floors have been converted from office space to a haunted forest, complete with fake trees, werewolves, and more. On the corner to the right is the old bank that any other day of the year operates as a museum, but tonight it's a hostage situation. Fake gunshots pepper the street, sending screaming tourists running for their lives, who were never in any true danger.

And between the two is a very dark, very empty bakery.

From the moment I stepped foot on Main Street this morning, I've been watching that storefront, waiting to catch a glimpse of the baker within. Every time I glance over there, my heart leaps with irrational hope that he'll change his mind. That Oliver won't let the magic win, that he'll stand his ground and serve his free samples the way he'd planned. I held on to that hope all morning and all afternoon, even as the bakery sat quiet and I reminded myself why that would be a terrible idea.

I look away, closing my eyes and letting my head fall back against the wall. Tonight is Halloween Eve, and we're no closer to breaking this curse than we were the day Oliver came to town.

"Amelia?" The tour guide pauses in the doorway, about to follow the last of their attendees out the door.

My head rolls to the side, and I can just make out their heavily lined eyes from over the register. "Yes?"

"There's a basket sitting out here. Do you want me to grab it for you?"

I straighten, brows furrowing. "A basket? Did someone lose it?"

The tour guide shrugs, glancing down near their feet. "I don't know. Looks pretty fancy. Like it's supposed to be a gift or something."

I stand, leaning over the counter to try and get a better look. Through the open door, I catch a glimpse of tissue paper peeking out from atop a wicker basket.

"Sure, bring it in and I'll see if I can figure out who it belongs to."

The tour guide sets the basket on the counter beside the register before tipping his hat at me and meeting his party on the sidewalk.

The basket is overflowing with stuff, the largest of which is a brand-new blanket knitted with thick fuzzy yarn that feels like a childhood teddy bear. Nestled in the top of the blanket, between layers, is a card with my name scribbled across the front.

> For your well-deserved staycation when
> your hosting duties are over.

The card isn't signed, but one glance at the rest of the basket's contents and I instantly know who it's from.

There's an array of things: A pumpkin-pie-scented candle sits beside one of those stuffed animals that can be heated up in the microwave in the shape of a black cat. Next to that is a bag of dark roast coffee and a box of butter-flavored microwave popcorn. There's a variety box of gourmet hot chocolate bombs sitting inside a ceramic mug with a ghost sipping coffee printed on the front. It's the handmade sweets at the front that give it away, though. In a bag is a stack of chocolate-orange cookies, and beside those is a container with a single chai apple cupcake.

The desserts Oliver planned to hand out tonight . . . before everything went to shit.

And right in the center of everything is a rose quartz heart.

We have love here in Ashwood Haven.

I don't doubt it.

Before I can stop them, tears are streaking down my cheeks. I wipe at them, trying to push the longing down and hide behind my customer service smile, but I can't. The tears continue to fall, and there's nothing I can do.

I gather the basket in my arms and bolt for the back of the store. Forget the customers, and the ghost tours, and the floating books, and the talking worm. I leave them all behind, refusing to look up as I bolt through the swinging door just moments before I completely fall apart.

I set the basket on a stack of boxes, staring at it through my tears before pulling out the cat and holding it close. There's a soft ribbon around its neck that's smooth against my fingertips as I start to rub it in an attempt at comfort. The stuffed animal smells like sugar and butter and spice.

It smells like him.

And that realization only serves to make me cry harder.

"Are you okay? I saw you run past and—" Lucy comes running through the door to the sales floor, frantically searching for me when she spots me crying into the stuffed cat. "Oh, hon . . ."

Lucy wraps her arms around me, pulling me close as my tears turn into muffled sobs against my new fuzzy friend. She runs her hand over my dark hair, softly cooing in an uncharacteristic attempt at comfort. But her concern doesn't make me feel better. Instead, it makes me realize how much of a burden I've become for no reason at all.

Oliver isn't someone I've been in a committed relationship with. He's not someone I moved in with, adopted a cat with, or started a life with. He was stepping out of my life as quickly as he had entered it days ago, but it was the realization that I hadn't really lost anything at all that made the whole thing so painful. I've walked away from years-long relationships with far less heartache as a result, because over time, it became clear to me that they weren't my person. The time had only served as a tool to teach me why walking away was the right choice for me. Did it still hurt? Of course—but it was nothing like this.

As someone easily drained by socialization, it can be easy to become painfully lonely. Being an introvert didn't mean I didn't want human connection; it just meant it took the right person to make that connection feel less like a chore and more like a safe place to land. A safe place to be unapologetically myself.

Losing Grandma meant I lost one of only two people in my life who gave me that freedom. I missed her crazy pranks and wild smiles, but I also missed my friend. Lucy is wonderful, but she's only one person, and it's not fair to burden her with the entirety of my social needs. She has her own life; her own hobbies, other friends. Now, I just have her.

And, over the last week, Oliver.

I hadn't realized how much my mask slipped around him. How easily I let myself be . . . me. Talking with him, being around him, didn't drain me. On the contrary, he'd made me feel truly comfortable and joyful for the first time since Grandma passed. This entire festival has turned into one overstimulating nightmare, and Oliver became my noise-canceling headphones. He didn't judge my desire to hide in my house. Instead, he remembered all the little things I told him and curated a self-care basket so I could enjoy every second of my self-imposed isolation.

That was more than I could say for any of those old relationships, and the fact that I didn't even have a chance to see where things could go pushed me over the edge that led to this breakdown. Finding another person I felt comfortable around was already rare, and now I didn't even get to see if we had a future together.

So yes, I cry over a week-long flirtation. I cry because of all the pressure I'd put on myself to act like someone I wasn't. I cry for all the pain my presence caused Oliver. I cry because I miss Grandma. I cry for everything I've put Lucy through, and all the things I depend on her for.

I just . . . cry.

Chapter Twenty-One

B *zzz bzzz.*
       Bzzz bzzz.

I give the notifications lighting up my phone a cursory glance before flipping it over to lay face down on the granite coffee bar.

"She's not going to stop," Lucy warns me, topping a latte with some quick foam art and handing it off to the customer waiting nearby.

I sigh through my nose, resting my chin in my palm as I flip through my book of shadows laid open on the counter. "I know."

I've almost gone through the entire book searching for any small hint at another way to break the curse. After hours of searching, I'm down to the last few pages and the last dregs of my hope. I woke up this morning with a refreshed determination to figure this out, to find the answer that felt so close and yet so far, but now I'm running out of ideas *and* time.

Today is Halloween. If we can't figure this out today, there's a good chance we won't have another chance until next year, and by then, it might be too late. It only took a year to run Oliver's grand-father out of town, despite having an established family business with roots as deep as the oak behind the gazebo. Oliver just got here. The magic could drive him out of town in record time, and our chance at resolving this could be gone forever.

Bzzz bzzz.

Bzzz bzzz.

I run my hands through my hair, suppressing the desire to pull it out by the roots, and groan instead.

I don't even have to look to know it's Stacy with a list of reminders, and several questions about when I plan to arrive, so I can give the commencement speech to indicate the start of Halloween. Tonight will be a night of downtown-wide trick-or-treating, costume contests, and more. Normally, I'd be giddy with excitement, waiting to see everyone—from babies in strollers to full-grown adults all dressed in creative costumes, both homemade and store-bought.

Our usual bowl of candy is already sitting on the counter by the register, waiting to be filled with the stockpile of candy I've been hoarding for weeks. I check the time, and there's only an hour until I'm supposed to step on stage yet again. I'm already nauseous at the prospect.

Thankfully, the store has been slow today with everyone preparing for tonight. I'm not sure how much longer I can main-tain my pleasant demeanor without breaking down yet again.

"Maybe we need to lean into the chaos," Lucy suggests, sipping on an iced pumpkin spice latte. I glance up at her from beneath my lashes, trying to decide if she's serious or not.

"What?"

She shrugs, her oversized flannel sliding further off her shoulder. "Things are already crazy. Maybe we should just embrace it. Go have a night of fun with Oliver and let the magic have its hissy fit and call it Halloween fun."

I stare at her. I know she's trying to be funny, but I'm struggling to find the humor.

"The magic almost traumatized an entire audience just two nights ago by siccing Saw on Disney characters."

Lucy grunts, stirring her drink with her straw. "Yeah, that was kind of a bummer"—a smile splits her face—"but you have to admit that would be such a funny crossover concept."

My hands fall to the counter with a *thump*. "You're sick."

"Oh, come on. Tell me you wouldn't pay good money to watch Saw try to trap the princesses, only for Mulan to kick his ass? Now *that* would be quality entertainment."

I shake my head, refusing to engage in this conversation any further, and flip to the last page of the book.

<u>Through The Veil</u>
A temporary ritual to speak with a loved one on the night the veil between here and the other side is at its thinnest.

"Oh my . . ." My head whips up, and for a moment, I can't even speak. I stare at Lucy with wide eyes.

How could I have forgotten about this?

"What? Did you find something?"

I spin the book around, pointing at the nearly translucent page. "The 'Through The Veil' ritual. This is it, this is how we ask Grandma what the lies were. *This* is how we fix everything."

Lucy shakes her head, watching me with concern. "Amelia, you can't. Absolutely not. Don't you remember Grandma telling us to never do this? She didn't even want us to know this existed."

I scoff. "Of course I remember, but what other options are there?"

Lucy pushes the book back toward me with a harsh glare. "We figure out a way to solve the riddle on our own."

My frustration rises by the second, because this is what we've been looking for. This is how we can get all the answers we need.

"We've tried that already, Luce. Not only have we tried that, but we've tried two different tried-and-true methods to break it, and it's only managed to backfire spectacularly. Tonight is our only chance. 'On the night the veil between here and the other side is at its thinnest.' That's tonight, that's right now."

I run to the front door and flip the sign to CLOSED, making sure there's no customers still in the store before grabbing the book off the counter and storming toward the back room.

Lucy is right on my heel. "Amelia, stop!"

I whirl on her, holding the book close to my chest. Tears are already starting to well once again, and I have to choke them down.

"No!" I yell at her, voice rising loud enough to stop her in her tracks. "I'm so tired of everyone telling me what I should and shouldn't do. Of everyone thinking they know what's best for me."

"And you think this is what's best for you?" She points an accusatory finger at the book still clutched tight in my arms. "Sacrificing a piece of your future? When the magic is already going crazy? You *really* think that is the right thing to do?"

I close my eyes, and I can hear Grandma's voice reach out to me from the past.

"Girls, I usually believe in enjoying magic and honoring everything our ancestors fought for and passed down to us. But you must

listen: Never, ever touch this spell. Do you understand? Magic requires balance, and to reach into the past, you must first sacrifice a piece of your future, and I promise you, it's not worth it."

A tear tracks down my cheek, dripping from my chin in a single salty drop.

"Yes," I decide. Even though the words are quiet, they don't invite any more questions; my mind is made up. "Yes, this is what I need to do."

Lucy's face falls, and after a long, unbearably loud pause, she nods. "Okay. What do you need?"

"What do you mean?"

She swallows hard. "The spell. What do you need? What do I need to grab?"

It takes me a moment to process what she's saying, but the moment I do, I jump into action. I lay out the book on one of the cluttered counters and run a finger down the page, truly reading the spell for the first time.

"First, we need something of Grandma's. Something personal. Something we can burn."

Fingers tapping against the counter, Lucy and I glance around in turn before she jumps up and runs out to the sales floor and returns in the blink of an eye. In her hand is Grandma's old diary.

She throws it down on the counter. "Nothing more personal than this, and I think we can both agree it'll feel good to watch it burn. What else?"

"Five candles, a burning bowl of cedar chips and moon-soaked salt, matches, and a piece of paper to . . ." My finger hovers beneath the words on the page, but I can't bring myself to say them around the lump in my throat.

The written name of the future willingly sacrificed.

Lucy nods, a determined glint in her green eyes. "Okay. I'll grab the candles and the paper if you get the rest?"

Silently, I agree.

It takes us a few minutes to gather everything. Before my phone can blow up with more texts from Stacy, we've arranged the candles in the shape of a pentagram and placed the burning bowl in the center, filled with the cedar chips and salt.

I wipe my sweaty palms on my skirt, looking over the setup one more time, ensuring everything's in place.

"I think that's everything. I guess . . . all that's left is to start. Do you have the paper?"

Lucy refuses to meet my gaze as she pulls the folded piece of paper from her pocket and hands it to me with shaky fingers. When I take it, she crosses her arms tightly across her torso, holding her middle tight. Her eyes never leave the paper as I pull out a pen and unfold it to write my name down, only to realize it isn't blank. I freeze, reading the name over and over again until it blurs together.

Lucy Graves

My mouth falls open, and it takes several thunderous heartbeats for me to find anything to say. "No," I whisper with disbelief. "Luce, you can't."

She shifts on her feet, rolling on the edges of her boots as she stares at the floor. "It's willingly given."

"But, it's your future. You have no idea what this is going to take from you."

"Look, just . . . take it, okay?" When I open my mouth to argue, she keeps talking over me. "You're right, we have no idea what it's going to take. Which means I should be the one to do it. You have so much going for you. You've got a guy who's clearly falling for you, a town that loves you, and a successful business. What do I have to lose? A job as a barista? A reputation as the town screwup? My family moved away years ago, and I barely talk to my mom anymore. You and Grandma were all I had, so I'm not going to let you take on one more thing when I can do this. Let me do this for you. You deserve to be happy."

"So do you," I whisper, tears burning my eyes.

Lucy gives a small, half-hearted shrug before she forces a smirk that doesn't quite reach her eyes. "Oh please, I'm never happy."

I stare down at her shakily scrawled name one more time, tempted to tear the paper to pieces. But I know Lucy, and I know that once she's set her mind to something, there's nothing that can stop her. Either I accept her sacrifice or she'll continue to fight me on this whole idea.

So with a heavy breath, I fold the paper back into a small rectangle, deliberately running a nail over the creases as I do, then I throw my arms around Lucy's neck and pull her close. Her arms tighten around me, holding me in a rib-crushing embrace.

"Thank you," I rasp, fighting down the lump in my throat that won't go away.

She pulls away, swiping at her eyes with the sleeve of her flannel, smudging liner and mascara across her cheek. "Yeah, yeah. I'm a good friend and all that crap. Let's get this over with."

I nod frantically, turning toward the circle we've created, the paper and diary held tight between my shaking fingers. Eyeing it all, my heartbeat starts to hammer in my ears, drowning out Lucy's fidgeting and my buzzing phone. One last chance to turn back. To change my mind.

I step into the circle.

I take a deep breath and close my eyes, muttering under my breath until the candles flicker to life one by one. All around me, I can sense the magic coming alive with a rush of energy. Though I can feel it there, the magic never passes over the bounds of my circle. Instead, it stalks around the edges, watching like a hungry mountain lion waiting to pounce.

I kneel before the burn bowl, and as I place the paper in it and light a match, I say the words of the ritual. They're thick and heavy on my tongue, sticking to my teeth and making it hard to speak at all.

"By willing heart a future sworn, a thread of fate is freely mourned." The flame of the match touches the paper, and the fire begins to consume wood, salt, and paper. "For love and soul, strong and vast . . ." I pause, watching the paper burn, and force the last words through my teeth, barely audible above my racing heart. "We trade tomorrow for the past."

The flames flare, growing in size as they're fueled by magic. I open the diary, which automatically opens to the October 31st, 1967 entry. The one with the curse scrawled across the bottom. I tear out the page and hold it to the flame.

"By bond and bone, by flame and thread, I call the spirit of one long dead."

A bone-deep cold washes through me, and I have to bite back the urge to shiver. Because when I look up, I'm met with familiar brown eyes that sparkle with mischief and love.

"Grandma?"

Chapter Twenty-Two

It takes all my self-restraint not to rush the phantom floating before me, to not pull her into a hug. All I want is to feel her strong arms around me once again and breathe in the scent of lilac and lemon, touched with the after notes of aged parchment. The scent I've associated with her since before I was old enough to put a name to them. Because the moment I go to grab her, I'll pass right through, and my heart will be broken.

The Grandma before me is only half here, transparent and lacking substance, but still so full of life.

Grandma reaches out to me, placing her palm against my cheek to cup my face. Though I can't actually feel her touch, there's a shadow of feeling . . . a memory of what it felt like before.

"Bug," she starts, the nickname slicing through my chest like a villain pulling out my heart. "Every day we spent together, I taught you lessons I fully intended you to ignore. But of all of them, why would you ignore this one and bring me here?"

I can't stop the sad smile that tugs at my lips, and I can hear the chuckle-mixed sob that busts from Lucy at the same time. Yes, Grandma taught Lucy and me about magic and all the rules that go along with it, but we both knew her rules were more like suggestions. She herself wasn't exactly a straight-laced witch, and she never expected us to be either.

I take a deep breath, preparing myself to delve straight into why I brought her here. There are so many things I'd rather talk about, so many things I'd rather ask, but we only have a few minutes before she'll disappear from our lives again, and I can't waste a moment of them.

"Oliver Blackwood, Richard Blackwood's grandson, has moved to town." At the mention of Richard, Grandma's face falls, a sadness I'd never seen from her before taking over her features until she's aged years right before my eyes. "Grandma, I need you to tell us how to break the curse. What are the lies? What do Oliver and I need to admit to, or own up to, in order to break this thing? What did Richard do that was so awful? The magic is trying to run Oliver out of town, and he hasn't even reopened the bakery yet."

Grandma sighs and bows her head. "It wasn't Richard who did anything. Richard was perfect; he did all the right things for the time. It was me, bug. I was the one who lied, and by the time I understood that, it was far too late."

I furrow my brows at her, trying to understand. "You . . . cursed yourself?"

Grandma shook her head. "Many things are missing from those diary entries, bug. I assume that's how you found the curse at all, since that's the only place I wrote it down." I nod, staying quiet to give her the space to explain. "We don't have much time, but I think you deserve to know the whole story. As you know, on Halloween night, 1967, I was hurting. As the last of my family, and newly broken up from my first and only love, I was more alone than I'd ever been in my life. I was desperate for one last chance to talk to my family."

Understanding dawns on me immediately, because I'm achingly familiar with the feeling she's talking about. "You did the 'Through The Veil' ritual," I whisper.

"I did," Grandma admits. "In a drunken fit of pain, I willingly sacrificed a piece of my future in exchange for a chance to talk to my mother one more time. I didn't realize until the ritual was over that the piece of my future I sacrificed was Richard. I didn't cast the curse, bug. The ritual cast the curse on me as the cost to see my mother. That's why I never wanted you to even consider doing this. Not even as a last resort. This ritual will take everything from you, and it will forever be my biggest regret. Seeing my mother, feeling her love, and hearing one last piece of motherly advice was wonderful, but it wasn't worth the love of my life."

I glance over my shoulder at Lucy. With her hand pressed to her mouth and the other crossed over her middle, she looks as though she's about to be sick. I want to run to her, to hold her and apologize, to promise I'll stay by her side until we figure out whatever the consequence will be for her sacrifice, but as soon as I leave the circle, Grandma will be gone and we won't have our answer. If I have any chance of helping my best friend, I need to learn how to break my own curse first.

When I turn back to Grandma, she's even more see-through than she had been before; she's already fading away, and I'm running out of time.

"What was the lie, Grandma? I need to know."

"'Til truths unfold, and masks descend,'" she quotes. "The lie was the mask. It was this facade I forced on myself. I thought I had to pretend to gain respect. That I had to be this strong, independent woman who needed no one and nothing for people to take me seriously. I let my pride get in the way of getting everything I wanted, simply because I thought other people's expectations of me were more important than what I truly wanted and who I truly was. I could have had Moonlit Pages, love, community, respect, and everything else. Instead, I was too narrow-sighted to let myself have it. But as you probably know, bug, I never let that mask go. Once I wore it, I never figured out how to take it off. I wore it until the day I died."

"I'm so sorry," I choke out, unsure what else to say. I can't imagine how hard that must have been for her. To spend her entire life pretending to be someone she wasn't, all for the sake of an image. All for the sake of the rest of the town and Moonlit Pages.

"Tell me," she says, leaning in and studying my face. "Why does it look like you haven't slept in a week?"

I sigh, rubbing my hands across my eyes as if the dark circles that have recently appeared can be wiped away. "This curse has been exhausting. It started out small, but every day, it gets worse and Stacy is freaking out, because she thinks I'm a bad host and—"

"Bug, you're hosting the Halloween festival?" Grandma's eyes are wide with horror.

"Of course," I tell her, unsure why that's the part she cares about. What about the people who have been hurt? The money lost? There are so many more important things to focus on. "It's Moonlit Pages's year to sponsor, and you aren't here to host, so I just . . ."

I just put on a mask and forced myself to step up so that I could be someone the town respected. I wanted to appear as though I could handle life without you and be the business owner the town expects.

Grandma shakes her head, her horror fading to a look of sympathy. "So you did exactly what I would have done."

In more ways than one, I think to myself, my thoughts reflected in her nearly invisible eyes.

"I never meant for you to follow in my footsteps. Not like this. From here on out, I want you to remember one last thing: Never live your life according to someone else's expectations, not even mine. You know what you need to do." Grandma presses phantom lips to my forehead. The ghost of love washes through me, and once again, I have to stop myself from throwing myself into her arms. "I love you, my little bug."

"I love you, too." The words are a barely audible whisper as she fades from view. A cold wind blows through the circle, taking the flames of the candles and Grandma with it, leaving Lucy and me alone once again. The breeze picks up the leftover ashes in the burn bowl and they flutter across the floor like sad confetti.

It takes a moment for me to gather myself, but when I do, the first thing I do is rush to Lucy. She's upright again, black liner streaking her cheeks where dried tears have fallen.

"I'm so sorry," I start, but she shakes her head.

"Don't," she chokes. "Don't even start. I can't . . . not right now. It was my choice, okay? It's not your fault."

I want to argue with her, but there's nothing I can say to change it now.

"Just go, okay?" When I don't leave, she gives me a small, sad smile that's entirely humorless. "We'll figure it out later—together —but the curse needs to be broken tonight."

Again, I open my mouth to argue, to tell her I'm not leaving her side, when my phone goes off again.

Bzzz bzzz.

Bzzz bzzz.

Pause.

Bzzz bzzz.

Bzzz bzzz.

I push a frustrated breath through my nose, torn between my need to stay with my best friend, who has possibly forsaken her future on my behalf, and my desire to break this curse once and for all.

"If you don't go now, I would have done this for nothing," she whispers, and that's what decides it for me.

"Fine"—I grab my phone and back away from her—"but we're going to figure this out, okay? I promise."

Lucy nods, but there's no glimmer of hope in her green eyes as she gazes at the burn bowl in the center of the floor. My feet almost stop, but she's right. If I don't break the curse, her sacrifice would be in vain. Grandma's curse wasn't an immediate thing; it took time to dig its claws into her life and tear it to shreds. We have time to solve Lucy's before it gets out of control.

So, against my better judgment, I turn and bolt through the sales floor and out the front door of Moonlit Pages. Weaving through the crowds of people, I duck and bob around children in costumes and parents bundled in warm coats as we all head toward Main Square.

I beeline for the stage, and for the first time, the sight of it doesn't turn my stomach to lead. Instead, I'm giddy because I'm not going to be the one up there tonight.

Stacy and Don are standing by the steps. Stacy paces with a phone to her ear as she calls me, my own vibrating phone clutched in my hand. The moment she spots me, her expression is somewhere between relief and rage, and I realize . . . I don't care.

"Amelia!" she screeches, hanging up the phone and letting her shoulders relax a hair. "Finally! We've been looking everywhere for you. We need to get you up on stage immediately. Remember, tonight—"

"No," I interrupt her, the word bringing a smile to my face.

Stacy stops in her tracks, finally looking at me. Truly looking at me. "No?"

I shake my head, feeling lighter by the moment. "No, I'm not going up there."

"But you're the host," she states matter-of-factly, as if I could possibly forget after an entire week of it.

I take a deep breath, because even though it's relieving to finally say it all out loud, I still have to fight the urge to cave beneath their scrutinizing stares.

"I hate hosting. I'm terrible at it, and I'm not going to do it anymore," I say in a rush, the words falling out of me faster than I can catch them, so I don't have a chance to take them back. When Stacy opens her mouth to argue, I turn to Don instead. "Will you do it?"

A wide grin splits Don's face, and he straightens, puffing out his chest with pride. "I'd love to!"

We both turn to Stacy, waiting expectantly. I wait for her to rant and rave about timetables and the importance of sticking to the plan, but instead, she lets out a sigh of relief. "Thank goodness. Don, get up there."

I'm stunned, mouth dropping open, but Don bounces with delight and rushes up the stairs, eager to greet the crowd.

"What? No fight, no 'remember to do this and that,' no nothing?"

Stacy turns her attention back to her clipboard, ticking yet another item off her never-ending list. "Sweetie, no offense, but you're right. You *are* terrible at this. I was doing everything I could to help because you were so insistent, but let's be honest, Don has been dying to do this for *years*. He's probably had this speech prepared for a decade now, waiting for his moment."

The magic around me swells like a tsunami and crashes just as hard. It ripples out through the town with so much energy that I stumble back as Don's voice booms through the speakers.

"Happy Halloween, everyone! It is my absolute pleasure to welcome you to our annual downtown-wide trick-or-treating," Don begins, explaining how every business and house within a mile radius will be open, handing out candy and decorated for trick-or-treaters.

I smile wide, my heart racing, because for the first time this year, I can look forward to Halloween—my favorite holiday. I'm absolutely thrilled, and I'm lighter on my feet than I have been in months. Before Stacy can give me any more directions, I turn and walk away.

A brisk wind kisses my cheeks, making my skin pebble with goose bumps, and as I go, I make a point of stepping on every crunchy, dead leaf I come across, simply because I can. My boots scuff against the brick, and I take the time to actually look around downtown.

Jack-o'-lanterns decorate storefronts, featuring everything from goofy expressions to intricately carved designs, like witches on broomsticks and haunted houses. Most businesses have lights strung up, too, each one in the shape of bats, ghosts, and pumpkins, dangling in the wind. Some have light projectors instead, and the antique store has a full movie screen in the window with various Victorian ghosts making scary faces at the people walking by.

Main Street is truly beautiful, swathed in red and orange garlands, lit up by colorful lights and fake candles.

And standing right in front of my store is a burly man in a long wool coat that covers his broad shoulders. Oliver cups his hands around his eyes, trying to peer into the dark. When he doesn't see anyone within, he steps back, giving the door a wary look that suggests he's weighing whether to walk away or plow right through it, until he notices me approaching.

He sighs with relief, running a large hand through his golden-brown hair. "There you are! Is everything okay? I felt whatever happened with the magic and ran right over to make sure nothing catastrophic was going on, but the store's closed and no one seems to be panicking and—"

Without a moment's hesitation, I cup his neck with my hand, push up onto my tiptoes, and pull him into a kiss. Oliver freezes beneath my touch, his hands held out to the side, away from my body, but he doesn't pull away. It's as if he's waiting for something to happen.

But there's nothing.

No magic buzzing, no screaming pedestrians. The pumpkins don't start singing, all the lights along the street stay on, and the plastic skeletons don't start dancing.

The moment he realizes nothing's going to go distressingly wrong, he relaxes into my kiss. His lips soften, melding against mine. His tongue swipes across the seam of my lips, and when I let him in, he tastes as good as he smells. Like butter, and sugar, and spice. One of his hands finds my hair, his fingers tangling in the strands as his arm wraps around my waist.

I curl my arms around his neck, closing any remaining space between us as the street melts away. I don't care if people are watching or if we're making a scene. I don't care that Mike or Simra or Ellie will give me a hard time tomorrow. I don't care if we become the subject of a hundred rumors and tomorrow morning's gossip. In this moment, it's just him and me—and no magic is getting in the way.

Eventually, Oliver pulls away an inch, breaking the kiss. He presses his forehead to mine to catch his breath.

"Fucking finally," he pants, and I giggle because I was thinking the exact same thing.

Chapter Twenty-Three

LUCY

I stand frozen in the back room of Moonlit Pages, shivers racking my body . . . as if not moving will keep the consequences of my choices from catching up to me. Maybe curses are like dinosaurs; they can't see me if I stand perfectly still. At least that's my logic, until a massive pulse of magic ripples through the town, pushing me back, and I'm given no choice but to stumble to catch my balance.

The burst of magic doesn't seem to touch anything but me and the ashes of the burn bowl I still haven't cleaned up. The ashes lift in a spiral, floating through the air before gently drifting to the floor in a scatter of gray and white.

That little push is what I need to start moving again, something like a weighted blanket settling around my shoulders. I start by gathering the candles in my arms, carefully balancing them as I reach for the stone bowl. As soon as I get closer, I notice something poking out from the charred wood and ashy paper.

I drop the candles to the floor with a clatter and reach for whatever is protruding from the remnants of the ritual that very well might have ruined my life. From the ashes, I pull out a perfectly folded piece of paper, untouched by the flames that devoured the other contents of the bowl. It looks identical to the one I wrote my name on, and when I unfold it, there are ten lines written in my own handwriting. My stomach sinks like a rock as I read the words of my newly decided fate.

From silent doubt, the fracture grows,
Where love once bloomed, now shadow sows.
A glance, a touch—yet none shall stay,
Their hearts like ash, blown far away.

The fault lies not in fate or flame,
But in the weight you dare not name.

'Til worth is claimed, not begged or sold,
And lies unlearned, no longer hold—
Then, the curse shall break,
And love may bloom for its own sake.

Epilogue

THREE YEARS LATER

Dear Lucy,

Yes, I know you think writing letters when I could just text you is dramatic, and no, I don't care. It's romantic and whimsical, and you will not take this from me.

I hope everything with the store and bakery has been going well since we've been gone. I know it's only been a week, but it feels like a lifetime. Oliver says I need to stop worrying because you've worked at Moonlit Pages forever, and Noah is more than capable of taking care of the bakery. I can't help it, though.

Ireland is AMAZING! I know, I know, I was so hesitant to agree to an international trip, but I'm so grateful Oliver talked me into it. Pub hopping around Dublin was truly like living in a book, and Giant's Causeway . . . I have no words. No. Words!

Which reminds me, the biggest news of the trip so far . . .

HE PROPOSED!! Right at the ledge of one of the highest points of Giant's Causeway. It was raining, cold, dreary, and absolutely perfect! I'm not going to show you a single picture until you get this letter so you can be surprised, but honestly, it's a scene straight out of a Highlander romance.

Anyway, give Noah our best. Remind him to call Oliver if he needs anything.

Love you,

Amelia soon-to-be Nova-Blackwood

P.S. Oliver told me you helped him pick out the ring. I can't believe you didn't warn me, or at least talk me into bringing cuter dresses! You're so dead when we get back!

Acknowledgments

A Witch's Guide to Surviving Halloween was never meant to be a story about deep self reflection and standing up for who you. It was meant to be a fun little Halloween romance to celebrate my favorite holiday. A side project to take my mind off the deeper stuff in the Thaumorian Legends. Alas, as per usual, I ended up writing the story I personally needed to read, as opposed to the story I had intended to write. With that said, I couldn't be prouder of how this story turned out!

As always, I must start my acknowledgments with my number one fan, always cheering from the sidelines: my husband. None of these stories I write would have been brought to you if it weren't for him. He's my second opinion on every decision, my shoulder to cry on when it gets too much, and my biggest believer.

Next, to my editor. I went a different way this time with my editor, which is always a big risk for an author. Our editors are like our coaches, and without a good one, the whole project can feel doomed. However, Wren was amazing and one of the best investments I made for this project. I couldn't be more grateful to have someone like her on my side.

To my cover designers, Ksenia, you're an angel. Truly. Anyone who followed the publishing journy for this book knows that just a week before my ARC release I decided to go with a new cover due to AI allegations. Ksenia was able to take my original order for character art and turn it into a stunning cover in the matter of days. I could not be more grateful.

To my family for being endlessly supportive. If my editor is my coach and my husband is my right-hand then my family is the cheering crowd filling the seats of the stadium. They are always first in line to buy my new books and have been unconditionally supportive.

Finally, to you, the reader. Without you, nothing I write would have meaning. A writer puts the story down on paper, but the readers breathe life into the words. On my short publishing journey I have aquired so many amazing readers that it's actually hard for me to comprehend. I don't know if I would have the courage to keep going if it weren't for you.

Forever grateful,

A.M. Eno

About the Author

Originally from Howell, Michigan, A.M. Eno travels full-time with her husband and cat. In 2017, she earned her Bachelor of Science from Black Hills State University, majoring in Psychology with a minor in Sociology. As a lifelong avid reader, she hopes to create worlds and characters that invite readers to fall in love and feel at home. She strives to write high fantasy series that are a safe space for people of all backgrounds.

www.authorameno.com